CTL

MARC

ATHENA

THE WATERS OF THIRST

THE
WATERS
OF
THIRST

Adam Mars-Jones

Alfred A. Knopf   New York   1994

THIS IS A BORZOI BOOK
PUBLISHED BY ALFRED A. KNOPF, INC.

Library of Congress Cataloging-in-Publication Data
Mars-Jones, Adam,
The waters of thirst / by Adam Mars-Jones.
p. cm.
ISBN 0-679-41941-1
1. Kidneys—Diseases—Patients—Fiction. 2. Gay men—
Fiction. I. Title.
PR6063.A659W38   1994
823'.914—dc20   93-35938
CIP

Manufactured in the United States of America
FIRST AMERICAN EDITION

This book is for Grier Smith:
blessings on Grier Smith:
bless Grier Smith

THE WATERS OF THIRST

I can almost see Terry at the supermarket check-out, unloading from his basket the convenience foods of self-pity, giving a tin of pears a maudlin caress. I see him placing the food in single file on the moving belt, advertising his solitude with a funeral procession of groceries.

It used to be trolleys in the car park, now it's the express queue. It's never more than one basket, and sometimes it's even 8 Items Or Less. The new signs actually say *8 Items Or Fewer*, after a campaign in the local paper against falling standards of grammar.

Terry's letting himself go. He's buying juice in little individual cartons, and he hasn't remembered to check with his finger as he pulls them from their display box, to make sure the straw that's meant to be there hasn't gone astray. He's one straw short. Someone else will arrive home with a bonus, two straws sticking to the waxy dabs of glue on the side of one carton. Someone else will be spoiled for choice.

It'll be days before Terry even realizes he's drawn the short straw, the straw that's so short you can't see it. Fate will see to it that he puts the defective item at the very back of the fridge; he'll have drunk all the other juices and thrown them away before he realizes what's wrong. Then he'll have to snip the corner of the carton and decant it into a glass. He'll have the worst of both worlds, the footling exorbitant portion without the childish pleasures of the straw. He won't be able to use the straw's sharp end to rupture the carton in its place of prepared weakness, then to draw the chilled liquid up the tube into his mouth, freer than glass users are to choose where exactly to experience the shock of refreshment – on his tongue or gums or cheek-linings. At last, in the moment after quenching, he won't be able to snorkel shamelessly with the straw for the noisy elusive last of the juice.

He doesn't know that yet. He stands dazed in his queue as it flows slowly forwards, thinking about me and about his life, and how they knitted together so well right up to the moment of unravelling.

The software in the tills is so advanced these days (as the check-out persons get more and more zombified) that when it comes to Terry's turn I wouldn't be surprised if it ran a search-and-compare programme – calling up the details of the last trolley-load debited to his swipe-card – and printed ON YOUR OWN? LONELY? DEPRESSED? on his receipt. And then the Samaritans' helpline number.

When I try to phone, I only ever get a message. The answerphone sounds as if it's underwater. It's not that I seriously expect to talk to Terry – that's not on the cards – but I do want to hear his voice, even recorded.

You'd think by now he'd have changed the message. It shouldn't still be my voice on the machine.

I took the dog back. Was that wrong? I paid for her, I trained her. I had the right. But perhaps it was wrong. I worry about that. I just couldn't bear him having her around for comfort. I'm not a petty person. I don't think of myself as a petty person. 'Baby come to Papa,' I said. She wagged her tail. Good girl.

I never thought we'd break up. We weren't meant to. I never thought I'd be resting in these unfamiliar arms.

It's strange. I'd hardly given monogamy a thought until I met Terry. I was younger then, of course, younger and taller. There just didn't seem a lot to be gained by trusting someone that far. Once the trusting started, I could see the sense of carrying on with it. I didn't see how it got started, that was all.

When I met Terry, I was actually seeing someone else and yes, even cooking for him once or twice a week in my little flat, but I knew well enough we weren't compatible. He kept saying he liked fish but not *fishy* fish, but in fact he'd shovel down anything I cooked. If there's a fishier fish than an Arbroath smokie I don't know what it is, and *that* went down a treat, served up with streaky bacon done crisp.

He said he was allergic to capers, but he couldn't get enough tartare sauce, which as you know doesn't have a lot else in it. So for all practical purposes I was single.

The crunch came when he prepared dinner for me, as he'd been threatening to do for a long time. He had often promised to make me what he described as his speciality, chicken stuffed with haggis, which always seemed to be a cruel thing to do to a chicken. No compliment to a haggis for that matter. But in the end he settled on doing something from a cookery magazine which had caught his eye on a news-stand. That issue happened to have a special feature on Pancakes and Batters, and he made toad-in-the-hole as a main course. Nothing wrong with that, in fact I was pretty much impressed. The recipe was a good one, using sage and garlic, and everything rose and crisped up nicely. It had the proper moist dryness of a Yorkshire pudding done the way it ought to be.

But then for pudding he served me something called a *clafoutis*. The recipe turned out to be from the same magazine, in fact the same feature – Pancakes and Batters. The best way I can describe it is as a toad-in-the-hole from which the sausages have been removed at the last moment and replaced with plums. So much for menu planning! Really, the whole thing had always been hopeless.

Terry and I didn't sleep together the first time we went out, which was unusual for the time. Mildly countercultural, you might say. It was 1977. Patience, dating, the waiting game, all that was a later fashion, a fashion that fear set. If you were courtship-minded before 1982, you were shy, old-fashioned or ugly, or some grisly combination. With Terry it could only have been shyness, but that wouldn't normally be a thing to hold my attention.

Pretty Terry, slim and sleek and, once you got

beneath his clothes, as furry as an otter. An otter with a big nose.

I don't even know why I agreed to another date. Yes I do. The anniversary of my Mum's death was just coming up, and I didn't spend that night alone if I could help it. If Terry hadn't been free that particular night – airline employees work some pretty unsocial hours – I don't think we would have happened at all. But on that night I was bound to be feeling vulnerable.

Mum was a dialysis pioneer, in the early days. Putting it that way makes my Mum sound like someone in a covered wagon – plugged into a dialysis machine to travel across the endless plains of the West. I suppose that's appropriate. My poor old Mum went west in a covered wagon of pain and disorientation. They hadn't worked things out yet, the way they have now. Mum spent ten to twelve hours on the machine, three times a week. I was young then, and to me it didn't seem like a medical treatment, it seemed like a punishment or a torture. Things are better now, I know, and there are all sorts of refinements coming along all the time.

Kids these days, with their high-flux machines and their Gore-Tex grafts. Two hours for dialysis! That's not kidney disease. That's a holiday.

Don't get me started. Anyway, the anniversary of Mum's death couldn't be anything but a bad time, and a night when I would be needing company. It helped that Terry liked to eat, and also knew about food, which isn't at all the same thing.

The first night I spent with Terry, I realized with a

shock that this was a man I might end up living with. I'm not interested in cock size, really I'm not. I suppose everyone says that, and only one in ten – one in a hundred? – is telling the truth. That's just the way it is. With me, it happens to be true. But you couldn't not notice what was in Terry's underpants.

He was, shall we say, noticeably undersized. He couldn't have been unaware of it. As I say, I really don't care about size, and I told him so, but he must have heard people say that time and time again and more or less despaired of meeting someone who meant it.

It ain't the meat it's the motion. It's not how big it is, it's how angry it gets. How long would he have to put up with them, the canting consolations of the securely hung? Knowing that some of them at least – and if so, which ones? – but maybe all, were thinking something quite different. *Why look, it's like a penis, only smaller. Is that a matchstick in your pocket, or are you pleased to see me?*

After we'd had sex and had cleaned ourselves up a bit, Terry fell asleep. I found that I was wide awake, which wasn't unusual even then, and strangely excited. It stood to reason that Terry didn't really want to play the field. He had nothing to gain by slutting around. What he wanted was to flirt, to flirt and to tease with his smile and his charm and his fierce little body, without having to come through with the goods.

Testosterone is an unforgiving vitamin, I mean enzyme, I mean – what do I mean? – hormone, and Terry never quite forgave himself for being undersized. What he needed was an excuse not to sleep with people. That way he could keep his status high. What he needed was a lover, not an open relationship but a real old-fashioned boy-friend. A tame monster. Somebody possessive and jealous, or somebody who didn't mind being thought possessive and jealous.

If he needed someone's possessiveness, for what I suppose are selfish reasons, he was bound to reward his partner with loyalty. Maybe loyalty of that sort wasn't the real thing, but I couldn't see what made it less worth having.

It didn't bother me that an arrangement like that would be selfish before it was anything else. Selfishness is fine. Selfishness is what makes people reliable. It occurred to me to think that this might be a way for trust to start.

None of these thoughts would have come my way, I dare say, if it hadn't been a morbid anniversary, a necessary time for thinking about limitation, and how to make the best of what you have inherited.

In an ideal world, of course, like most people, I'd go to bed with strangers and wake up either alone or with people I know. That's normal. What it isn't, is *workable*. Things with Terry might be workable.

I can't say that Terry saw it that way at first. He was grumpy in the morning, when he woke, and it turned out that I had made his nipples sore when I had played with them the night before. You'd think he'd be grateful that I'd found a point of focus – two points, if you're going to be pedantic – some distance away from the part of him that made him feel so inadequate.

He wasn't good at talking about sex, not then and not ever, so he found it hard to convey his meaning. What he said, rather desperately, while he got dressed, hunching his shoulders to delay the moment when his shirt made contact with his abraded chest, was indirect. He said, 'You don't have to be that way. You don't have to be so rough.' And then, 'You were much more . . . sensitive earlier on. Last night.'

I didn't get it. I couldn't work out what he was trying to tell me. Last night? Earlier on? That's when I'd got up to the tricks that he was getting so huffy about. If he'd been able to say straight out, 'Just be as sensual in bed as you are at the dinner-table, and we'll get on just fine,' it would have saved a lot of time. I took ages to catch on.

We'd eaten out the previous evening, and I'd ordered an artichoke for my starter. So I imagine Terry had seen me tenderly scraping the oiled flesh from the fibrous leaves with my bottom teeth, with all the greedy tact you could want in a lover. Now he was trying to tell me that was the way to treat him, as something delicious.

From then on, whenever we started to make love, I tried to visualize his pretty chest gleaming with vinaigrette, and after that I don't think he had anything to complain of. I learned how to savour him.

Terry kept his side of the bargain. His modest penis was the linchpin of our whole arrangement, but that was never said in words. We weren't big on words, but then we didn't need to be. We never even had arguments. We never exposed our friends or our dinner guests to the slightest disharmony.

There's a moment in a dinner party, isn't there, when you realize that all is not well between your hosts. It's nothing crude, it's not that they're using packet gravy or anything. I've tasted gravy made almost to competition standards in homes where, the same weekend, someone's hand got shut in the knife drawer really quite nastily.

It's more subtle than that. You notice that your hosts are both in the kitchen at the same time, leaving their guests to fend for themselves. It only happens for ten or fifteen seconds, but it's happened all the same and it means something. You can be holding a glass and looking out at someone's garden, glass in hand, and you can see that there's a good show going on for another week or two, and a few promising patches coming in that'll look really nice next month, but in between there's nothing, just nothing. And you wonder what was going wrong in the household when the planting was being planned.

It even happened that Terry and I were served the same menu at the same house, the exact same menu, at two dinner parties in a row. We exchanged glances of pure shock. What could our hosts have been thinking of? There's only one explanation possible. The first time we were there, or after we left rather, our hosts had such a bad set-to, over the washing-up maybe, that their normal routines got disrupted, and neither of them remembered to make a note in their diaries about what food they had served us. So when they were planning the second occasion, they had no hospitality archive to work from, and they had to trust to luck, which is always fatal in matters of hospitality.

Terry and I weren't like that. We kept our promises to each other. When we started going together, way back in 1977, Terry showed me the last skin magazine he had bought. It was called *In Touch*, the April '77 issue, and these days it looks fairly ridiculous. Even naked, the models seem to be wearing the ill-advised clothes of the period, and they're all in need of a damage-limitation haircut. Terry not only showed me the magazine, he gave it to me. He didn't care what happened to it. He expected me to throw it away, although I'm sure he didn't give it much thought. He had no use for such things any more, now that his life was settled, now that he was on his way to being happy, and he never bought another.

Terry didn't, but I did. In that April issue was an advertisement for another magazine and a photograph of a newcomer, a rising star of the flesh trade. He was billed under the slogan *Introducing Teen Talent*, but I imagine he was a little older than that in real life. It wasn't a lie, it was just a technical category. He was still playing those parts, the porn *ingénu*, the kid in the locker room, hitch-hiker drawn into a threesome.

I sent off for the advertised magazine, which had a lot more pictures of the young man. I remember one tableau in particular where among the tangled legs you could just glimpse a kitten, peering inquisitively up at the camera from under a piece of furniture. I felt sure it was *his* kitten, somehow. The up-and-coming porn star's pet kitten! The stuff of dreams. The magazine also contained an advertisement, towards the back, for yet another magazine, which for rather more money would show him with a variety of partners. I sent off for that too.

Peter Hunter. It's a ridiculous name, pretentiously plain, but by now its associations are so complex, so profound, that I've forgotten that. After all, if you were starting up a pop group that was going to change the world, roughly the last name you would choose for yourselves would be The Beatles. I remember seeing The Beatles on *Thank Your Lucky Stars*, as it happens, a matter of weeks after they'd dropped the Silver from their name, and I thought, what twerps. And what a stupid name, which luckily we'll never hear again. I must have been about fourteen then, I suppose, and going through a very censorious phase.

So. The Beatles. Peter Hunter. Proof that you can hang on to a name, and still change it, just by changing what it calls up in people's minds.

In due course Peter Hunter made videos as well as doing photo sessions for magazines, but I never bothered to buy them. I wasn't stupid enough to send off for them to America, where the technology isn't compatible, just to find out I'd invested good money in some of the most expensive groaning in the history of the world. I could have had access to transcribing equipment through work at a later stage, if I'd put my mind to it, but I never gave it a thought. I wasn't interested. As time went by, it may be that some of the fuck books were really only selected stills from the videos, but still I was happy with them. I liked the idea that what I was looking at was only a selection of moments, and having to imagine the moments between.

Peter Hunter got a look on his face towards orgasm – you can see it right from the beginning of his career – which for me was his trademark, the sign of his uniqueness. His co-stars, and there were plenty of them early on, while he was working his way up the star system, tended to look sly or calculating as they approached the moment of coming, as if they were being paid by the millilitre and had worked out in great detail what they were going to buy with the money. Peter Hunter wasn't like that. Even when he was only one of a group of car mechanics (I'm sorry, I can't bring myself to say auto mechanics, let alone *grease monkeys*) at the edge of the action, and they hadn't even bothered to dirty his overalls, so they looked brand new, when he was still the equivalent of an understudy in the chorus, waiting for some big star to fall and break a leg, Peter Hunter always looked as if he was in the grip of overwhelming sensation. Interior avalanche.

There was a purity about him that wasn't to do with being above the body, above the physical. You could tell the difference early on in his career, when he was dressed as a religious novice for some scenario involving seminary high jinks. It wasn't that he looked bad, or even awkward, out of place. He looked fine, but the costume didn't add anything to him and what he was.

At his best, he had the innocence of a big animal, a dog or a horse.

It isn't easy getting porn in Britain, as I'm sure you know, but I had a stroke of luck. A friend of mine from drama school days got a job at the Traverse in Edinburgh. I say he was a friend, but I never seemed to have people coming to see me on first nights in pub theatres and saying 'Darling you were wonderful,' the way you're meant to. What I got was more like 'Darling you were almost good.' Apparently you could always tell it was me. Well of course you bloody could! My name was right there in the programme, in case people had any doubts.

Well, actually I knew what they meant. I never pretended to be that sort of actor, the sort who won't take no for an answer and drags audiences bodily off to ancient Greece or the Arctic Circle.

They don't tell you this in drama school – in fact this is a great secret I'm letting out of the bag – but when you come right down to it most of what passes for acting is no more than text-based wheedling. You're wearing your costume, you've learned your lines, you've blocked out your moves, but whether it's a gun or a bunch of flowers you're carrying on stage, really you're down on your knees in front of the audience, pleading with them to make it all happen. 'Please believe in me,' you're saying. 'See, I've even put on a little bit of an accent for you. What more could you want, really? Come on, start believing. You know you won't enjoy yourself until you do. Why waste the price of your ticket? Shocking what they ask these days, isn't it? And all down the drain unless you believe in me – please? – with my costume and my moves and my lines and my little bit of an accent.'

There are only ever pleaders and kidnappers in the profession, and some of the pleaders can be very persuasive. Over the years they learn to do some really top-flight wheedling. Kidnappers are always rare. They probably aren't even alive when they're not acting. The rest of us drift in and out of the profession, giving what we can to it, taking from it whatever we can get.

I did what I could, on stage. I had my moments. Anyway, I got my own back on at least one of my lukewarm theatre friends. He wasn't getting a lot of work himself, any more than I was, and he'd started doing some photography as a sideline. Eventually he had an exhibition of snaps at his local public library. Do I have to spell it out that if you've been pointing your camera at local buildings and people for long enough, the only way you can *not* get an exhibition at your local public library is if you've gone and left the lens cap on? So I walked round his little exhibition, and then congratulated him heartily, shook him warmly by the hand. 'Wonderful,' I said. 'Genuinely impersonal work. When I look at your pictures, I really feel I'm being shown the world as it is. Local buildings, local people. No distortions, no subjectivity. There's no you anywhere here. Congratulations!' It was the sort of acclaim I was supposed to be working for, on stage. And of course he looked absolutely crushed.

But this wasn't the friend who worked at the Traverse, though he called it the Travert. Travert like 'pervert', though I think a traverse is only the Scots for an alleyway or a short cut. Anyway, I was in Edinburgh one Festival time and staying with him, and we took a walk along Princes Street in the late evening. A bagpiper outside one of the department stores caught my eye, some opportunist with a kilt – pipers are never local at Festival time, locals would die of shame, they invariably turn out to be from Toronto or Wellington – and I said, quite casually, 'this probably won't mean anything to you, but that could almost be –' and he cut in, without a beat, as we theatre folk say in our complex technical language, 'Peter Hunter'.

As it turned out, we weren't really members of the same fan club. He was pretty much omnivorous in the matter of pornography. I specialized in Peter Hunter, and he specialized in everything.

He had an astonishing collection. He told me that customs officials in Scotland just weren't interested in policing the mail in search of offending printed matter, unlike their cousins down south. They let well alone. Did you know that? North of an irregular line drawn on a map, the buildings might be grey granite but what you got through the post could be just as colourful as you wanted. Perhaps Scottish customs officials were heirs to a different philosophical tradition, or perhaps sin made them feel so wobbly they couldn't bear to think about it, but it came to the same thing in the end. They let well alone.

All the same, I like to think that the authorities north of the border are showing the secret softness of their nation. There is a lenience beneath all that austerity, an almost appalling softness. So many thousands of men pretending to be alcoholics, with a glass in each hand at all times – pint of heavy, dram of Grouse – so that you can't miss what they're doing. And all to be forgiven their easy tears. They wipe their wet eyes with the backs of both paws at once, the heavy and the Grouse alike forgotten. For a moment they drop the pretence that addicts them, and softly they sob. Scottish taps, too, grate and squeak when you try to turn them, and then gush out from softly poisonous lead pipes such soft water, sending the driest dagger of soap into ecstasies of lather.

The soft permissive North, then, leaving well alone, allowing filth to circulate. This was a revelation. It was as much of a thrill in its way as finding a quiet little restaurant where they really know what they're doing, and don't expect to become millionaires in a matter of weeks. You'd have to be mad to tell your friends.

My friend the Pervert from the Travert offered to let me use his address for my imported Peter Hunter material, and he would even send along anything relevant to my collection from the magazines he subscribed to himself.

It wasn't as strange an offer as it might seem. He owed me something. In the normal course of events you'd expect him to be pushing work my way, but I dare say he was another friend who thought my theatre work was almost good. He wasn't about to do anything silly, like hire me.

By that time, I could more or less cope. I'd accepted that I wouldn't be spending much longer in legit theatre, that I'd end up somewhere else. I didn't yet know where, that was all.

So I was content to accept the peace-offering he made. Actually, it was wonderful. It was like having my own erotic cuttings service, free of charge. I doubt if anyone in the country has a more complete collection of Hunteriana than I have.

Over the relevant period, I practised sex exclusively in its safest forms, fidelity and fantasy. I was faithful even to my fantasy. And still I can say that I suffered along with the world.

Terry and I chose each other when there were only breezes blowing men like us together, or apart. After a few years there were high winds blowing every which way. Winds rattled every door, winds blew down every chimney and tested every window, and people were blown together and blown apart, blown away, without any warning.

People who were caught in the open when the wind got up, or took shelter too late in little nests that they just threw together, tend to exaggerate the tightness of our timing. We weren't canny about it. To hear some people talk, you'd think we'd sniffed the wind and smelt the sexual recession while it was still some way off. But it wasn't like that. It's not as if we sold up at the last minute, realizing our assets on the eve of a stock market crash. We were already established in the cosy hutch of our monogamy when the Big Bad Wolf started trying out his lungs on the neighbourhood.

It just so happened that Terry and I closed a door on the world at a lucky time, but we never meant to lock it. It was always in our minds, at first, that we could decide to open it, any time we wanted to, and just walk out. And then there was something waiting outside that neither of us could face. Then we were grateful to turn the key in the lock, to slam the bolts home, in the knowledge that we were safe if we stayed put where we were behind our door.

Meeting when we did, our monogamy wasn't Aids-induced, but I don't see how I can deny it was Aids-maintained. Terry and I were suited well enough, but compatibility is always an approximate thing, don't you think? Strict fidelity makes things better, and worse. Monogamy is a style of life, not a standard of conduct. It doesn't mean that you behave well, necessarily. It only means that there is no alternative within the rules to your being forgiven by your partner, sooner or later.

In practice I can only remember my offences against Terry, not his against me. What was the worst thing he did? He called me, affectionately, by a nickname I hated, but that was hardly his fault. Early on in my second career, which turned out to be the real one, doing voice-overs for advertisements on television, I overheard a couple of engineers referring to me in a way that paid tribute to my professionalism. It was true that it took me very little practice with each assignment to find the particular distortion of the throat that rings true for a particular product, and to generate the abstract conviction of voice that the job depends on. It came easily to me. So I was well enough pleased to overhear these two technicians refer to me as 'One-take William'. Except that I realized, a moment later, that they'd actually said something a little different. From their suddenly guilty expressions and obvious embarrassment, they'd said something distinctly less flattering. It took me a moment to work it out.

It's funny. There are certain moments when you realize you have a sort of flight recorder somewhere in your head. Presumably it's working all the time, but you're not usually aware of it. Your mind knows much more than it knows. I imagine in the future that as part of any autopsy they'll take the flight recorder, your own personal black box, out of your head and wire it up. They'll project it on to a screen or transcribe it on to a tape, and someone in a white coat will point to a particular bit and say, 'There's your problem.' That's why he didn't look both ways before crossing the road, or whatever.

Anyway, this was one of those moments when you're somehow able to rewind the tape, just a few inches, and you can play it back to find out what you've missed. I found out what it was the technicians had called me, what I'd failed to pick up in my hunger for a compliment. They'd called me 'One-take Wilma'.

That evening I told Terry what I'd overheard, but in the form that I'd first understood it, as an unmixed compliment. I was anxious to pass on any good opinions I got for my work, since it was through Terry's charming and flirting with an advertising executive at the check-in desk that I'd got my break in the voice-over business in the first place. I wanted to show that I'd earned the business that had started out as a favour to Terry – even, perhaps, as a bargaining chip in a doomed campaign, on the part of some Super Club Class smoothie, to get into those tight little trousers and find out what was there.

Terry knew I didn't like abbreviations of my name, that I didn't think of myself as a Bill or a Will. He wasn't about to call me Willy. Heaven forbid. So he more or less pounced on what I'd told him as an acceptable nickname, something that gave him a little scope for endearment. Quite often from then on he'd call me 'One-take William', or just 'One-take'.

At first I didn't mind. I had mixed feelings, but that's the way feelings come, mixed. I suppose what I felt about what the engineers had said to each other was a rankling glow. That's as close as I can get to it. I thought the rankling would wear off and the glow would last, but I was wrong about that. It turned out to be the other way round. The professional compliment came to seem a trivial thing, as my confidence grew, compared to the hurtfulness of the casual disparagement.

But of course Terry didn't know that. He went on using the nickname in all innocence, not knowing it set my teeth on edge every time. And I couldn't tell him why.

My offences against Terry weren't major matters, I
suppose, but they weren't quite as innocent as that. In
my mind, they cast a longer shadow. For instance. Oh,
it's so stupid. When we were supermarket shopping, I
would sometimes hold a tin of fruit near my ear and
shake it, putting on a shrewdly judging expression. I
used to make a hot fruit salad – not the subtlest dish in
the world, as I freely admit – in theory a Jamaican recipe
using plenty of rum and sand sugar ('pieces', if you can
get it), and most of the fruit could be fresh but you
needed a syrup base, and tinned pears are really not
bad. There's no shame in buying the odd tin of pears.

I have to admit that on one occasion I even picked up
the tin I'd selected just as we were getting to the head of
the queue at the till, shook it next to my ear and screwed
up my face as if I was thinking better of my choice. Then
I dived back down the aisle to exchange it for another
one no different, leaving Terry to shepherd our trolley
through.

I came back in triumph with my new selection, just in
time for it to be rung up with the rest of our purchases,
shaking it contentedly next to my ear as if the pears
inside were making music. And all because I knew I
could make Terry blush, every time. He wasn't from a
comfortable background, and he had once told me that
his mother would do exactly this trick with the tins. She
thought she could tell from the faint gurgle of the syrup
which tins were properly packed to the brim with fruit,
and which ones had been topped up unduly in the factory with juice or water. She used to audition every tin

on the shelf, while little Terry squirmed and wished he was dead.

It was cruel of me to remind him of the distance he had travelled. In all our years together, I saw Terry cry only twice, once when his father died and once when he was describing an obscene stew of pork liver that his mother used to make.

I'm sure every couple could tell similar stories. I hope so. Terry and I got to know hundreds of couples over the years, and I don't think we were unusual. Most of them were gay, of course, but there were some straights in there too. Some of them may even have been married, though I don't particularly remember. It takes all sorts, doesn't it?

Some of the straight couples were colleagues of Terry's. There are quite a few heterosexuals in the airline business, mainly in administration. I'm always surprised by how many straights there are, and in all walks of life, not just in the obvious professions.

If I'd had to rely entirely on Terry's colleagues for entertainment and social life I think I'd have gone mad. There's a limit to the number of times you can magic your lips into a smile when someone tells what passes for an amusing anecdote among airline folk. Example: a unit – that's a passenger – presents her ticket at the check-in counter. She's asked if she'd like a window seat. She replies, 'Are you mad? Can't you see I've just had my hair done?' How we laughed.

Over time I learned certain general rules about airline personnel. Flight attendants complain about their feet and their smiling muscles; ground staff complain about their backs, and the fingers they strain repetitively working the computer keyboard. It's a fixed thing. Perhaps it's even how the jobs are allocated. Perhaps at interviews applicants are asked whether they would rather complain about their feet and their smiles or their backs and their fingers, and are gently steered towards the speciality that gives individual talents for whingeing their fullest rein.

But most of our dinner guests, thank God, were our neighbours at various addresses, as we unhurriedly improved our standing in the housing market, in the years when money had momentum.

Not all of our neighbours, of course, were the sort you ask to dinner. Some of them wouldn't have come even if they'd been asked. One very sporty neighbour used to acknowledge us on his morning or evening runs, gasping out 'Good . . . mor . . . ning' or 'Good . . . eve . . . ning' as evenly as his overstretched lungs would allow. Then there came a time when he would only nod, and we understood that he had grasped, or been told, the nature of our relationship. It was only a small indication, and by itself it wouldn't have been conclusive, but I spotted a piece of circumstantial evidence that pretty much clinched it.

Up to that point, he and his girl-friend (they weren't married) would hang up their washing to dry on a sort of carousel in the yard, visible from our kitchen window. Now I noticed that though she was as unselfconscious as ever in what she hung out to dry, he had

started to censor the laundry bag. He had, well, privat-
ized one particular area of the wash. He still yielded up
his running shorts and Y-fronts, boxer shorts and even
quite skimpy knickers to the public gaze. But he no
longer trusted us to see his athletic supports – let's face
it, his *jockstraps*.

It wasn't particularly that I scrutinized his contribution to the drying carousel – I didn't use fieldglasses
or anything – but the colour spectrum of a straight
man's wash is normally so narrow that even quite
mildly daring choices stand out as if they were
caught in actual beams of black light. I don't remember
anything more flagrant than an item in battleship
grey, possibly another in dark purple. Nothing so *very*
compromising.

I don't know how he solved the problem he set himself by withdrawing from the public domain the manly
pouches that would have inflamed our deviant eyes.
Perhaps he sent them out to be laundered. I prefer to
think that he put them in the washer as before, but
hung them indoors to dry. I like to imagine the living
space festooned with strings of jockstraps, like Christmas decorations. Elasticated garlands out of season.

Perhaps after we moved on up the mortgage ladder,
which in those days seemed to go up into the skies like
Jack's beanstalk, this sensitive athlete went back to his
old habits right away. Or perhaps he waited for a month
or two to satisfy himself that the new residents were of
good moral standing, a probationary period, before he

ran up on to the clothes-line once more the shy bunting of his intimate sportswear.

Other neighbours down the years would have jumped at the chance of seeing inside the house – only they were never going to be invited. There was one woman I remember, at one of our addresses, who more or less ambushed the postman if he'd rung our doorbell and waited as much as five seconds. She couldn't wait to sign for parcels and packets, wanting to shake them or X-ray them or just hold them up to strong light.

She was always sweeping the pavement outside her front door. Then she started sweeping outside our place, too, 'just to be neighbourly' as she put it, but really so that she could scan our windows for goings-on and be sure of catching the postman. Still, she was a fearless cleaner when she got to work, whatever her reasons for laying claim to our stretch of pavement. She'd even tackle dogshit.

She turned out to be a Jehovah's Witness, and sometimes she wouldn't wait for the postman, she'd play postie herself. She'd pop leaflets through our letterbox off her own bat, with copious annotations. *True*, she'd write against some passages – many passages – and sometimes a fuller comment, like *The POPE is WRONG as EVER*, or *unclean = hated of God*.

She was harmless. It was no different, from her point of view, from us neglecting the garden. Then she would have given us tips on borders and hardy annuals. She would have slipped seed packets through the door. She would have rung the bell and shyly offered us the use of her mower, her rake or her secateurs.

It just so happened that the garden she saw running to seed was our souls, mine and Terry's, and none of her business. All she wanted was for us to be completely different from the way we were, and then she'd have lost interest. She'd have found another hobby or another challenge for conversion. But apart from that, she was all right.

After we moved, she didn't give up, she just took to mailing us her homilies and annotations instead of delivering them herself. They followed us through several changes of address. We never did work out how she kept track of us for so long. Perhaps there are Jehovah's Witness moles in high street estate agents. I even almost missed the leaflets when they finally stopped coming. Actually, I found myself thinking, Wonder what happened to her?

The airline laid on a hotel room for Terry near the airport when he was on unsocial shifts, so it wasn't crucial where he lived. He didn't say 'airport', of course; even airlines cling to their little bit of jargon. He'd say 'hub'. And I'd say, 'Aren't I your hub, Terry? Aren't I your hub?' And he'd say, 'No, Gatwick's my hub. You're my lover. You're my One-take.'

I too could be fairly flexible about location, once I'd found my niche in the voice-over market-place. With two incomes – his more reliable than mine, of course, in the early days – and a willingness to anticipate fashion in your choice of area, it's surprising how quickly you can afford a bit of garden, the double garage that becomes a virtual necessity for you, and some mildly ambitious remodelling. You get spoiled, don't you, when things are going your way, and for a while there's no such thing as a luxury. Everything is a necessity, whether it's a guest room that never sees a guest or spare goblets for the blender, so there's always at least one clean even if the recipe is very elaborate.

Now the bottom has fallen out of the housing market, of course, but for a while back there the going was good. I think Terry and I got the same sort of pleasure from seeing the potential of a dowdy suburb as we did from serving Chilean Cabernet Sauvignon, when our friends were only just summoning up the courage to risk Bulgarian.

Handling drink socially can be a problem, of course, if you can't touch any yourself. Terry indulged moderately, but I had to steer well clear. I remember seeing an edition of the *Antiques Roadshow* once, where somebody brought along a peculiar object to be valued by the experts. Terry and I used to watch that programme regularly. When videos came along, we preferred to record, and we turned watching the playback into a little bit of a ritual. We'd watch it without the sound, and try to work out from people's expressions how much they'd been told some heirloom or market-stall bargain was actually worth. Then we'd wind back the tape and test our guesses. Neither of us knew anything much about antiques, but it was surprising how close we could come to the right figure, often, just going by facial expression and gesture. The signs were rarely obvious – no excitement-spots on thrilled cheeks, no hugging of the treasured thing, the vindicated purchase. There was just a suppressed facial earthquake. English orgasms of greed or disappointment.

Anyway, one evening on the *Antiques Roadshow* a woman brought along something called a tantalus, a sort of lockable case for decanters. The expert explained it was so that in olden days your servants might be able to see your supplies of drink, but they couldn't get at them without your permission and the key – Tantalus being the Roman god of thirst or some such. I even forget what the woman was told her heirloom was worth, because the word 'tantalus' set something off in my mind.

A tantalus doesn't have to be a locked pair of decanters. For some people an open bottle of wine can be a tantalus, even a bit of anonymous liquid at the bottom of a glass can be a tantalus. Anything that you must have, and may not. Anything that your body craves and your mind knows you must do without.

Still, whatever your personal difficulties, I do think your duty to entertain your guests' palates extends beyond food. Sometimes I have to say that our guests weren't exactly discriminating. I remember one couple who were our neighbours at one stage, Jenny and James, who knocked it back so freely that for once in my life I had to serve some white at room temperature. For some reason you can get away with exact calculation about food portions, and people understand it's not practical to ask for more, but if you hesitate to open another bottle you're dicing with death socially. An empty plate says nothing, it makes no statement, but an empty glass is always a hint or an accusation.

All the same, I was grudgingly liberal with the booze on the evening Jenny and James came to dinner. They were an odd couple, but I suppose it takes one to know one. Perhaps there are only odd couples. Certainly an *even* couple is a distinctly sinister-sounding idea.

I remember Jenny saying she was surprised when James took a romantic interest in her, because they'd been pals for a long time without any apparent tension. More than once he'd put her into a taxi after a party, or even accompanied her home if she had passed out. He would put her chastely to bed. Once he'd even cleaned her up after a vomit.

Jenny had warned me when I made the invitation that James had high blood pressure, and had been warned to live more healthily, to cut down on saturated fat and so on. The two of them worked for the same brokerage firm, but in fact she seemed to be the higher flier, and it wasn't doing her blood pressure any harm at all. It seemed absurd that James should be so stressed at barely thirty, but of course I didn't know the background then. I told Jenny that I could at least promise that the dinner would be as low-sodium as James wanted it to be, since I never cooked with salt.

Jenny also asked me, rather disconcertingly considering I hardly knew her, if I thought she should be 'taking precautions'. I could hear the inverted commas in her voice. I suppose I was her only gay friend, and that's why she asked me, but I was slow on the uptake. I said of course she should take precautions, unless she was planning on a family. Then I realized what she was trying to say. The end of the world had been widely preached by then, in the leisure centre, at the dry cleaners. Everybody knew something, but I suppose in another way nobody knew anything, and it can't have been easy knowing who to ask.

I had to tell her that I was the last person on earth to give her advice. I've never worn a condom in my life, that was what I told her. I'm not about to start now. What I actually said was, 'My dear Jenny, the closest I've come to putting on a condom was when I made my own sausages – and *that* wasn't worth the trouble.'

Anyway, I'd taken Jenny's hint about the menu, and I had looked through all my cookbooks for something rich and healthy, complex in the mouth but bland in the belly and the bloodstream. If you know anything about it, you'll understand that's the culinary equivalent of squaring the circle, but finally I managed to work it out. I found an elaborate fish recipe with plenty of taste and no fat, only olive oil, and clove after clove of heart-soothing garlic. Good old Jane Grigson.

I was feeling lighthearted when I carried the finished and rather spectacular dish into the dining-room – I always get a lift when the garnish is scattered at last and there's nothing more to be done – and I couldn't resist a little gentle teasing of this odd couple, this couple as odd as we were ourselves. As I carried in the serving-dish, I said, 'We only ever serve the female monkfish in this house. It's one of our little rules.'

'Oh, and why is that?' asked James, with a now-you've-done-it look in Jenny's direction, as if she was bound to have something to say about that.

'Yes, why is that?' Jenny put in, squaring her shoulders for a set-to.

'Well . . .' I explained, 'the male monkfish is only two inches long, you see, so they tend to slip through the nets,' and Jenny laughed so hard she choked on the last olive from the canapé tray. She said something I didn't quite catch, about throwing back the little ones.

After that, I thought James was a little truculent, which may just have been the gin and then the wine. It isn't easy keeping track of your guests' drink-induced mood-swings when you're abstaining yourself. I don't think James even noticed that the entrée was chosen with his needs in mind. It was like a savoury compliment flamed with brandy. Of course I know that not everybody sees entertaining the way I do, every plate piled high with sociability and commitment, but you'd think Jenny would nudge him under the table – kick him, even – to get him to be more gracious.

It was a good long while before we were invited over to their house, and I couldn't help feeling, when I realized that there would be ten of us at table, that this was one of those oh-God-who-do-we-owe occasions, where you pay off your social debts wholesale without really expecting your guests to get on. I felt that our hospitality was being repaid in a diluted form, somehow, without being appreciated for what it was. There was plenty of drink on offer, of course, which didn't do me a lot of good. The dinner itself was almost defiantly convenience food, top-of-the-line supermarket product admittedly, but still hundreds of miles away from the real thing.

I've always been a better host than guest, even at my best, I suppose that's obvious, and I couldn't quite control my tongue. I'd planned to say, 'Delicious, you must give me the recipes,' with just a hint of sarcasm if Jenny cared to pick it up – she made no great claims for herself as a hostess, and she could be self-mocking – but then I found myself adding, quite clearly, ' – or the bar-codes, anyway,' which was going too far. Terry got us out of there in seconds flat. It was a classic display of a common social manoeuvre, the hurried marital retreat.

On that occasion, I noticed James was wearing a pony-tail. It seemed such a badge of yuppie rank that it never occurred to me he had been sacked shortly before, while Jenny had kept her job in the same establishment. The pony-tail was a little tassel of compensation for the privileges he had lost. It didn't suit him, but pony-tails don't suit anybody, they're not meant to suit people, so that didn't signify. Jenny was trying to keep his spirits up – which may have been one of the reasons for the party – but from his point of view I suppose she was part of the problem, since every day she was commuting to what until recently had been his place of work also. With the loss of his salary he'd had to cut back on his cocaine habit more or less from one day to the next, which can't have helped. Jenny didn't approve of drugs. She kept him on a tight rein as soon as she was in a position of power and could get away with it.

Then one evening he rang our doorbell. Terry answered the door to him. James explained that he had locked himself out, and asked if he could come inside to wait until Jenny came home. We brewed him some tea, but it was noticeable that he wouldn't come into the house proper. He was only happy in the hall. Perhaps he thought that gay men were certain to pounce on an unchaperoned male unless a line was drawn at the start. People have such funny ideas. But it may simply have been that the hall was where he felt he would be imposing on us least. All three of us ended up there, perched on chairs that weren't really for company, but for company's coats. James mentioned rather casually that the glaziers would be paying a call in the next day or two, since he had broken a window with his hand.

It should have occurred to us that the only way you are likely to break a window-pane with your hand is by giving it a good punch, but I have to say that it didn't. Still, we were only neighbours, and virtual strangers at that. By this time, though, Jenny couldn't afford to blind herself to the reality of James's mental state, and she arranged for him to visit a psychiatrist.

On the day fixed for his appointment, James went up to town instead. He went to the kitchen-equipment section of a high-toned department store, and he bought a very beautiful meat cleaver, the finest and heaviest in the entire Sabatier range. Perhaps he had moved in his extremity beyond considerations of thrift and extravagance, or it may have been less dramatic than that. Perhaps he simply hadn't yet got into the habit of economy, even in the case of a purchase that would only be used the once.

Back at the house, he made a serious attempt to cut his left wrist. He seems to have thought in terms of cutting the hand off, to judge by his choice of the cleaver and also, I gather, the action he used, closer to chopping than to slitting. He got as far as the tendons. Then his mind cleared in a remarkable way. He found that he was in great pain, and not at all depressed. There was no longer any fog in his head, but there was blood running down his arm.

He phoned the emergency services and told them what he had done. There happened to be an ambulance station just round the corner of the street where we all of us lived, but perhaps they were out on another job at the time. At any rate, his call wasn't answered with the speed he had expected. Perhaps his sense of urgency was only a hangover from the indomitable yuppie impatience. But he was also in steadily increasing pain, and less depressed than ever. He ran out of the house to greet an ambulance that was nowhere to be seen, and the front door clicked shut behind him.

So it happened that he rang our doorbell for the second time that week. He wasn't waving around his gashed wrist, which was a mercy, or Terry would have passed out. He had wrapped a tea-towel round it. He explained quite calmly what he had done, and asked if he could come inside to wait for the ambulance. Again he didn't want to come any further than the hall.

There was a ring of bloodstains round his mouth, and further staining of his neck and even his hair. It didn't seem a good time to ask if he had tried to drink his own blood. Perhaps he had only been hoping, unrealistically in the face of the damage he had done to himself, to stem the flow of blood, or to bring on clotting with the mild coagulants in saliva.

Hospitality is how we make casual relationships sacred, but this was a challenge. Terry and I retreated to the kitchen and considered our options, talking in whispers. We knew better than to offer James anything to eat or drink, even if he had asked for something. For some people, at certain times, a tantalus can be something as basic as a glass of water, or a cup of tea.

Still, we both felt a powerful urge to do something that would endorse his choice of our hall as a place of refuge. It seemed important to find some way of acknowledging his gesture, however involuntary it was in reality. There were other doorbells in the street, and he had not passed us over in his need for shelter. He accepted us in this crisis, even if his feet had merely repeated a journey familiar to them from a few days before, when he had last locked himself out. No matter. He had accepted us, and we needed to show that we in our turn accepted him.

Eventually, whispering in our huddle, we decided we should give him another tea-towel for his hand. He had made mention of the hand in his hysterically calm speech when we had let him in, but had said nothing about the stains round his mouth. Best in the circumstances to pretend that we'd seen nothing, that there was nothing to see, though it would have been doing the ambulance men a favour if we'd cleaned James up a bit before they arrived. A tea-towel was the most tactful offering.

There followed a not very dignified wrangle, I'm afraid, about which tea-towel to offer. On that particular day, the only really clean tea-towel available was one from the National Trust for Scotland, not easily replaced. It seemed unlikely that something lent under these circumstances could be claimed back without giving offence.

I should say in our defence that it was the sort of emergency that is likely to find any household unprepared. In the end I went to the laundry basket and retrieved a tea-towel from there. It wasn't clean, obviously, or it wouldn't have been in the laundry basket, but it was no more than moderately soiled. It was a present from someone, and it had nothing more worth keeping printed on it than a recipe for Irish potato bread.

We took it in to James, and wrapped it round his wrist over the towel that was already there, and which was by now pretty thoroughly stained. I wouldn't have let him unwrap his wound and put our dirty towel in contact with it. In any case, Terry would have fainted if he had. He was already being tested to his limits by the marks round James's mouth, though strictly speaking what he minded wasn't actually blood but the wounded flesh that does the bleeding. I'm not squeamish myself. With my history I could hardly be that.

It was only a few seconds after we had wrapped our symbolic welcome round James's arm that the ambulance came for him at last. I saw it arrive, flashing its lights but not sounding the siren, and I ran out to tell the ambulance men that we were looking after their passenger. Again, James gave a calm and concise account of his attempt at self-mutilation, and they helped him into a wheelchair.

As they wheeled him out on to the street, I said I'd call Jenny, and asked him for her phone number at work. He was in shock by this time, and couldn't remember it, but he asked me to get his wallet from his back trouser pocket. He stood up shakily, the ambulance men supporting him, and I fished for the wallet, while Terry watched from the porch. This was an intimacy that went beyond hospitality. I could feel the mortal shiver of his buttocks. James could have asked the ambulance men to find his wallet, and by asking me I felt that he was expressing his acknowledgement of the tea-towel and what it represented. But perhaps being in shock meant he was not in any condition to express nuances of acceptance and rejection. I was shocked myself at the time. But still I sensed a personal meaning in his request.

When I pulled out James's wallet from the sweat-drenched pocket, I thought I was looking for an address book or diary with Jenny's number in it. But of course they had been co-workers until recently, and what he wanted was one of his old business cards.

Only when James was standing shakily up in the wheelchair, and I was fishing through his trouser pockets for his wallet, did I realize what was different about him. Oh, of course he'd gone mad and he'd had a go at his wrist with a cleaver, and he'd smeared his face with blood like some voodoo priest of the suburbs, but I mean something different. At some time since I'd last seen him, James had cut off his little pony-tail. A symbolic yuppie castration had gone before the more ambitious piece of self-inflicted damage, but then he hadn't been satisfied for very long by the sacrifice of symbols.

I waited till the ambulance had left before I made the call. Terry came down from the porch into the street to join me. It would have been crass for us to wave as James was taken away, but somehow it seemed necessary to stand there rooted, smiling faint encouraging smiles, as if we might in fact wave at any moment, until the ambulance moved off.

When I phoned Jenny, I listened carefully to how her voice sounded when she reacted to my news. She seemed not to be shocked, though I don't think she was actively expecting it either. I dare say what James did to himself was one of those things you realize after the event had been looming for some time. Most things are like that. I told Jenny which hospital James had been taken to, and she went there right away. I told her to stop in later for a cup of tea or a bite to eat. I thought she might need fortifying for what was waiting for her at home, but I underestimated her. She didn't look in on us. She coped on her own.

She told us about it later. The blood was almost all on a rug, which she simply threw away. There was the bloody great meat cleaver lying where James had dropped it, of course, but there was also the bag from the Conran Shop nearby, with the receipt still in it. So she cleaned the blade with boiling water and took the cleaver back to the shop. She exchanged it for a coffee pot and a lasagne pan.

That was when I realized how strong she was, strong enough to visit her lover twice a day while he was in hospital (there was quite a bit of work to be done, they kept him there a week and a half), and then to cut him out of her life as quickly and cleanly as possible.

Every time the doorbell rang after that, I thought instinctively it was James bringing us another mutilation to look at. Some fresh stump. But it was usually only the vicar doing his little bit of meddling. What do they call it? Outreach.

I could never take vicars seriously, I'm afraid, as a breed. Terry and I were even in the habit of using the phrase 'More tea, Vicar?' to mark the end of sex, smoothing the transition back to the demands of the day. After that, it's hard to talk to real vicars without feeling the urge to giggle.

This particular vicar would always make a bee-line for the least comfortable chair, making it clear if only for his own benefit that he wasn't there to enjoy himself. But if he mortified his bottom, at least when he was on his pastoral beat, he indulged himself pretty freely in other departments, as far as I could see.

Vicars never quite get shoes right, have you noticed? Even the chummiest of them don't quite dare to wear running shoes, but they go as far as clumpy items like Cornish pasties for the feet – more orthopaedic-looking than casual.

I could never quite work out whether this particular vicar wanted to welcome Terry and me into the community, to make clear that there was room for us in God's house, or to see pictures of naked children and dogs. Somehow in the middle of all his sincerity he struck a conspiratorial note. Still, Terry thought he was on the level, which counted for something.

I wish I found it possible not to ask people into my house just because I happen to dislike them. I watch myself open bottles of wine for them, pour savoury nibbles into glass dishes for them, knowing there'll be nothing left in half an hour but salt-dust, even if they've said they won't have anything to eat, thanks just the same, even if they've said they don't want to put me to any trouble.

I'm incapable of buying inferior wine for less favoured guests. I just don't have the plonk reflex. Even if I could buy it, I know I could never serve it. Some hypocritical gene of hospitality makes me say, 'It's no trouble,' and open a bottle anyway, knowing they'll say yes then, if only to 'keep you company', though of course they'll be drinking alone.

Perhaps that's one of the ways I compensate for not being able to touch a drop myself, by never allowing other people to fall below a certain level of quality. If I can't indulge my appetite, at least I can celebrate theirs.

This particular vicar, though, needed no encouragement. He never said no to anything he was offered. I remember one evening he started a story about his holiday on the Isle of Wight, which I succeeded in deflecting with some cashews. He had met some young man in a camp site, but I managed to head the conversation off before he got round to telling us whether the encounter was a prayer meeting or a grope. It really made no difference to me whether they went down on their knees or each other. I didn't want to be hearing about it either way.

As it was, I had to watch while the vicar wolfed my cashews and slurped my wine. In his hands, cashews were not a finger food. They were a fist food. I suppose anyone who eats nuts has to choose whether to pick them up and eat them one by one, which looks prissy, or to scoop them in numbers into the palm of the hand and then more or less fling them backwards into the mouth while throwing the head back, which looks piggy. The vicar plumped for piggy, every time. All I could think of as he threw down those salty nuts, in between hearty slurps of my better than adequate wine, was what a dehydration orgy this was. How much processing he was taking it for granted his body would do, while he tried to bring the conversation round in a circle, relentlessly back to his holiday snaps in prose.

Perhaps he had a weak head for alcohol, I don't know. Perhaps the high quality of what I was sullenly pouring into his glass made him drink more than he otherwise would. At any rate I remember one occasion when he looked straight at me and said with a surprising earnestness that as far as he was concerned we, William and Terry, had the same status as a couple as anyone whose union he'd blessed in church.

His glass was empty, and I dutifully fetched the bottle of wine from the sideboard, but I wasn't going to be drawn into an intimacy I didn't want, just like that. I said, 'I'm afraid you seem to be under a false impression, Vicar –'

'Bob.'

'Vicar Bob. Terry and I don't sleep together, you know, which seems to be what you're implying.' This was true, and had been for years, but had more to do with Terry's unsocial hours and my insomnia than anything else. A spirit of pure mischief made me add, 'Still, Terry always makes sure I have a proper cooked breakfast, don't you Terry?' and Terry went very quiet. Anyway, I managed to shut Vicar Bob up for that evening at least. I made him back off from whatever queasy declaration he was working himself up to make.

I wonder why I minded the vicar and his approaches so much more than the Jehovah's Witness lady, who I suppose was pretty much persecuting us, when you get down to it. But with the Jehovah's Witness lady, I could just let it go past me when she was on a rant, let it all go by. With Vicar Bob I had to intercept him time and time again, before he could recruit me for all sorts of things I didn't want to be part of.

He had a trick of starting a sentence with the words, 'I'm not speaking as a priest now, William . . .' and I learned to be ready for him, and to say, 'Oh but you are, Vicar Bob, you can't help it. You worked for it, you may as well enjoy it.' And he'd flinch a bit, but he'd turn it into the sort of smile that says you enjoy the rough-and-tumble of outreach, and are well able to look after yourself.

Nature is the best casting director, that's what it comes down to, and Vicar Bob could never have got away with playing a vicar on stage, with his red lips and a growth that needed shaving twice a day. What could he have been on stage? With a little moustache, ineffec-tual officer in the trenches (dies of wounds in Act Two). And without? Understudy at best.

Vicar Bob was very big on what he called the Aids Ministry, which was another phrase I learned not to let go by without a challenge. So I'd say, 'Oh, round here I expect you get more call for your Arthritis Ministry or your Hypothermia Ministry or even' – thinking of James – 'your Redundancy Trauma Ministry. This isn't Earls Court, you know.'

It was Terry who said he thought Vicar Bob was a worried man, and was looking for people to confide in. He didn't say this the night of Vicar Bob's embarrassing conversation about our 'union', but the next morning.

People who sleep together have bedtime rituals, I dare say, but Terry and I had our rituals in the morning, or the start of the day, anyway, if Terry's shifts had knocked him out of the conventional orbit of days and nights. I'd wake him up with a cup of tea, and afterwards we'd talk.

Terry wasn't religious in any formal way, though he had his little magic spells and compulsions. He'd been brought up to think that peacock feathers were unlucky, and of course I just happened to have an Indian fan made of nothing but. I'd inherited it from my Mum. I started to say, I've had it for years, and nothing bad has happened to me, before I realized that there ·'as another way of looking at it.

For an airline employee, though, Terry was actually rather rational. God knows, I've come across enough superstition in theatrical circles, but there's never been anyone to touch airline employees. The silence in a dressing-room if you happen to mention *Macbeth* is a loud and bustling thing compared to the silence I made, once, round my dinner-table by saying the word 'Lockerbie'. I suggested to Terry afterwards that maybe we should take a leaf out of the thespian book by not referring to the disaster directly – using a roundabout phrase, perhaps, like 'the Scottish crash' – but he didn't seem to think that would help.

But Terry did have his own little rituals, even if they weren't exactly superstitions. He needed to touch things symmetrically – if he'd touched something with his right hand, he needed to repeat the contact with his left – and also in groups of five. So if his right hand grazed something by mistake, he needed to touch it four more times, and then five times with the other hand, which tends to look awkward however unobtrusively you try to do it. Lots of people are the same way, I'm sure, but Terry was a little different. With him, it only happened at work, and it was all to do with work. If he didn't complete his ritual, it wasn't that he was afraid something would happen to him. He was afraid that something would happen to the passengers who were passing through his hands. He was terrified that the pilot would crash the plane, except that airline people don't say that, they say something that's a little magic spell all by itself. They say 'drop the plane'. Terry was afraid that the pilot would drop the plane unless he got all his touches right.

Air travellers are insecure people, which doesn't help. For instance. If they died on holiday, or their loved ones did, they'd want to come back home to be buried, but all the same they don't fancy flying in a plane that has dead bodies aboard.

In fact, though, you've never been on a scheduled flight where all the passengers have been alive. The recently dead have a sort of momentum that keeps them travelling. You can demote them to the hold, you can treat them as luggage that you hope will get lost, but you can't stop them from coming along. It's just that the airlines have learned not to say 'dead bodies', they don't even write 'dead bodies' on dockets and manifests, instead they use the word *hermans*, which is code for 'human remains'. Then everybody's happy.

But it's the same when airline personnel are dealing with air travellers. It's easy to make them jumpy, and hard to reassure them. They don't like stewardesses to have any human characteristics at all (Terry would kill me for saying that), and they don't like ground staff to be twitchy. They don't like their Passenger Service Agents to tap their fingers in irrational rhythms against the edge of a passport or the side of a check-in desk.

It was a problem for Terry. It's not the sort of thing that you can just wish away. But what I thought might help would be if he tried to let the superstition settle in his feet. Perhaps his hands would behave sensibly if his feet were allowed to be as irrational as they liked. He could flex his toes inside his shoes whenever the urge took him, and no one would ever know. No one would look at him oddly. On top of which, he could have the satisfaction of knowing that every toe-flex was automatically a gesture divisible by five.

There was always the possibility, of course, that Terry's obsession would spread to his toes without leaving his fingers. Still, I thought it was a risk worth the taking. And it worked. Terry learned, not to deny his compulsion, but to shift it around, and for all practical purposes be free of its inconvenience. After that, his demeanour was impeccable as he escorted his units down the plush tunnel from the boarding-gate to the plane. When he closed the plane door on them, and heard the stewardesses lock it on the other side with a hollow clunk, it wasn't a compulsion that made him, every time, lay the flat of one hand on the door – one hand, and one contact – in a gesture of futile protectiveness and blessing. It was a voluntary act, a proper prayer.

That was as formal as he got. Terry wasn't a church person, but he took Vicar Bob's part all the same, when we talked about his visit. Perhaps Vicar Bob called round sometimes when Terry was in and I was out, and perhaps Terry let him finish one of those sentences that began, 'I'm not speaking as a priest now . . .'

It was the morning after Vicar Bob's visit, and I'd brought Terry his cup of tea in bed and everything that went with it. We were lying there in the afterglow, and he asked me, Didn't I think Vicar Bob had the look of a worried man? A desperate man, even? I told him I hadn't really thought about it.

Terry said I should stop thinking about him as a vicar. Terry's idea seemed to be that Vicar Bob wasn't old and wasn't even, technically, bad-looking. And Terry asked, What did that suggest to me?

Nothing, I told him. I didn't care. I said I wouldn't want him taking his dog-collar off in my house, thank you very much, even if he turned out to be Mr Bull-Necked Universe underneath it.

Terry told me that wasn't it. I didn't understand. All Vicar Bob wanted to do was bare his soul, get something off his chest. It was pretty obvious he was gay, he said, and I said I'd worked out that much. Well, he said, he couldn't settle down with a partner, the way we had, the Church would turn a blind eye to some things but not to that. So the chances were that he'd . . . *indulged*, that was Terry's word, on his holidays, before anyone really knew what a bad idea that was. And now he needed a lot of reassurance. Where did I think he was going to get it?

Maybe he wanted to take a sock off, Terry said, and show us a coloured blister on the sole of his foot that had been losing him sleep, and have us laugh at him, tell him he was being a big silly to worry about it. *Big silly!* Then he would burst into tears and be comforted. Who else could he talk to if not us?

I had to say that I still didn't care. I preferred the older idea, that they were there to comfort us, however little we wanted it, but at least it wasn't the other way round. I just felt there was something slimy about Vicar Bob – slimy as that felt-tip they hand you in the fishmongers, to sign your cheque with. And then I shut Terry up good and proper by saying, 'Don't you think I've got enough on my plate? Don't you think I've got troubles enough of my own, without running a counselling service for troubled clerics who should have known better when they misbehaved on holiday?' To which there was no answer.

Terry's bedroom was always where we had sex. My bedroom was where I kept the Peter Hunter archive. Terry knew I received regular packets from Edinburgh, and he must have guessed they were flesh magazines, but he never asked. I didn't tell him anything, because to do that I'd have had to show him pictures of Peter

Hunter. It wasn't that I was being possessive, just that Terry could have interpreted what he saw only one way. Peter Hunter had a good healthy skittle between his legs, an engine of some power even when idling, and Terry would have seen my whole collection as a sort of overcompensation for his own shortcomings. It would be no good saying, which is true, that a substantial cock is no more of a necessity for a porn star than a good speaking voice is for an actor – it's a qualification, yes, but not the be-all and end-all. Terry couldn't imagine a fantasy that wasn't about cock size. For him, that's what a fantasy was, a dream of big cocks, cocks to put his in the shade, cocks to put *him* in the shade. Cocks to blot out the sun.

I could have put in a special request with the Pervert from the Travert for a portfolio of the truly outsized, if I'd thought it would make Terry feel better. He could have seen for himself that Peter Hunter occupied only a modest middle ground of endowment. Believe me, some of those boys that I saw in magazines that happened to contain a fleeting snapshot of Peter Hunter were like those special dishes you see on restaurant menus – Porterhouse steak or whatever – marked 'for two persons'. Backsides quailed, and even mouths could only make a lateral approach, not gorging on a lollipop but shyly nibbling at corn-on-the-cob. To me, those photographs had a powerful undercurrent of unease. It was like watching someone practise parallel parking with a Zeppelin. I imagined somebody with a walkie-talkie just out of shot, shouting desperate course corrections. Sighs of relief all round when the thing was safely docked, with no damage to property or livestock. God knows what Terry would have made of it all. On balance it was kindest to keep my collection private.

In a career that lasted just under fifteen years, Peter Hunter took part in well over a thousand sessions. Some of the early magazines were collector's items even when I bought them, but you can never really tell what will become valuable, so it seemed more practical to keep them all in transparent plastic pouches.

In any case, pornography in a protective cover brings with it an extra layer of transgression, as if this wasn't your bedroom at all but a dirty bookshop in which you were furtively browsing. Seeing how far you could go before the management sent some heavy over, a policeman of arousal to breathe down your neck.

Sometimes I was able to get a duplicate of a particular item, and then I enjoyed the luxury of having a reference copy and a reading copy, for the research I was doing one-handed. With the reading copy I could allow myself liberties that would be out of the question with magazines where I had no duplicate, flicking back and forth between images even at the risk of tearing a page. It was possible to eroticize the difference of state between two copies of the same magazine, one so pristine and innocent, the other matter-of-factly dog-eared and stained. Even without being opened, the contrasting copies rehearsed the drama of defilement and release that took place impartially on the pages of each.

My collection would have been worth a lot of money

to a fellow enthusiast, but to me it represented something beyond price. A few times I swapped one rarity of which I had more than one copy for another that was missing from my collection, but those were the only times I had to put something like a fixed value on my treasure.

From early days, I felt that Peter Hunter was different, that he was more than just a body and an image. It wasn't just that there was some kind of dumb magic in his eyes. At the beginning of his career I suppose I sympathized with him, and identified with his struggle to leave juve roles behind and establish himself as a leading man in his own right.

As time went on, though, I noticed something else. There was nothing second-rate about the magazines he was in. Sleaziness I've come to love, but I can't abide anything shoddy. When he was still in the back row of the porn chorus, unable to set his own standards, it always irritated me that there would be newspapers spread out on the floor, as if the concrete of the fantasy garage needed to be protected from staining. I realize that I'm a member of the last generation to be print-oriented, and people younger than me would never think of being distracted from their arousal, but I could never see those newspapers without trying to read what was in them. I'd rotate the magazine on its axis, or turn it upside-down. I'd let myself be side-tracked from my excitement by what would always turn out to be money-saving grocery coupons from the American Midwest. Why the Midwest? I deserved better.

In Peter Hunter's mature work, nothing of that sort ever happens. The sessions in which he appeared had qualities, technical qualities, that put them above the competition. The lighting was good, for one thing. But more than that, someone involved had an eye for – I'm embarrassed even to mention it – continuity. I know it's something you're not supposed to notice. Your eye is supposed to travel hot and headlong from organ to orifice to organ. But I notice discrepancies, and they break the spell for me. Some beefy kid is being interrogated down at police headquarters, and you turn the page and suddenly he's not wearing a shirt any more. The handcuffs are still in place, but the shirt is gone. Meanwhile his captor has somehow made his own trousers disappear, while the gunbelt has fastened itself magically around his bare hips, all in the course of a single masterful snarl. And you find yourself thinking, *Who are you anyway, the Houdini Sluts? I want smut, not escapology*, and this is not a sexy thought.

If there was such a thing as a continuity boy for porn films, that would be my dream job. You can picture me, can't you, consulting my clipboard and saying with just a hint of priss, 'If you look at the rushes, Mitch, I *think* you'll find that Bruno's bandanna should be knotted a little more *fiercely*, if you get my drift. And I'm afraid Dale's tattoo is starting to run again.'

But with Peter Hunter's photo sessions I had the strange feeling that someone actually was attending to those details, making sure the whole thing was consistent. I mean, I'm not stupid. I know the whole thing's a performance. If Peter Hunter ejaculated early on in one session, and did the same thing with the same splendour a few pages later, I knew that the scene would have been staged in two sections, so that he could recover his strength. It's not like the theatre, when you can have given everything you've got at the matinee, and still you have to find something for the evening perf. But it was still important, to me at any rate, that you couldn't see the break in the filming from anything in the images themselves.

In one photo session, Peter Hunter is playing pool in a bar when the action starts. He's from out of town and doesn't know that he's playing on a table that's reserved for some rough studs. He comes twice before the bike gang leave him drained on the baize. They pull his T-shirt roughly over his head, and they pull his jeans down, but he's wearing a watch on his wrist from beginning to end of the scene. One day I was curious enough to get out a magnifying glass and look at the watch whenever it was in shot and could be read. I was amazed. The hands of the watch seemed to move in plausible small increments, just as if the whole lovely rape was being photographed in real time. I know there are some people who would get turned on by the idea that their hero was some kind of incredible sperm factory. Me, I was turned on by the idea that there was someone who really cared about the details, who had anticipated the scrutiny of my magnifying glass and was determined not to be caught out by it.

I started to imagine that Peter Hunter had a Svengali,

an older man who'd had a long and distinguished career in photography, and prepared everything with an obsessiveness that could only be a form of love. Then one day my eye came to rest on the last page of a magazine, where they put the information about copyright. I always loved the fact that American pornography is confident enough about its legitimacy to invoke the protection of the law. I saw the phrase THE PURE NET given as always as the copyright holder. The little phrase which was as familiar to me, by then, as my own name.

But on this particular day, perhaps because I'd been doing a crossword earlier on, I started to rearrange the letters, first in my head and then on a scrap of paper, as if I was working on an anagram. And I came up with PETE HUNTER. I was astonished, though I was also a little puzzled. He was always Peter Hunter in the magazines, never Pete, and the slight untidiness seemed somehow out of character. Then I realized that the little R in a circle, after THE PURE NET, meaning Registered Trade Mark, was actually part of the anagram. PETER HUNTER it was.

It hit me all at once. Peter Hunter owned the company that exploited him. If this was the sex industry – and I'd heard it described in those terms – then Peter Hunter was a sex industrialist. Yes, he was the exploited product, but he was also the board of directors. Putting it another way, he was like an old-fashioned actor-manager. I felt elated, more than that I felt proud, as if in some irrational way I personally was ratified by this new information. It was like opening the paper and finding that someone you grew up with has made it in some major way. One of us, one of *us*, has done something wonderful.

There was also, I don't deny it, a definite buzz about being part of an elite. Of all the thousands of men who had bought Peter Hunter magazines, how many had realized the significance of the company name? Peter Hunter would take his clothes off for anybody, but to us, the watchful few, he had peeled a little slice of his mind.

After that, I started noticing quite a few things. In the magazines I received from Edinburgh that weren't actually Peter Hunter productions, but reprinted images of him, I noticed that THE PURE NET® was always credited in tiny letters by the side of the photograph. Most pictures were uncredited, and I'm sure the bulk of them were simply pirated, reprinted without fee or permission. That was when I realized that Peter Hunter's professionalism didn't just extend to the continuity. He had a little empire. It was clear that his company retained legal counsel, and whoever they were they certainly seemed to know their stuff.

I even started to wonder whether Peter Hunter hadn't trained as a lawyer – that anagram had a definite graduate feel to it – and perhaps had started doing dirty pictures as a way of paying for his tuition. Then I realized that this was me backsliding into fantasy, calling up half-remembered images of young men with Clark Kent glasses playing with themselves in the deserted stacks of the law library – until they are surprised by the sports coach, grizzled but virile, coming to look up some base-ball litigation. I suppose, if I'm honest, I have to admit that my earlier theory, of the Svengali who was Peter Hunter's director of photography and continuity mas-termind, also had its roots in pornography: the youthful uncle from the Camera Club, the darkroom and what goes on there.

Terry didn't know about the Peter Hunter archive, but he knew what was the size and shape of my secret, which was as good as being in on it. I didn't pretend not to have a secret, which is the hurtful thing, isn't it, in a relationship. About something much more damaging, something that thoroughly threatened the future, I told him absolutely everything, right from the start.

I didn't actually go up to him on first meeting, hold out my hand and announce, 'My kidneys are polycystic. It's a congenital condition. It killed my mother. Things look a little bleak in the kidney department,' but I came pretty close. Admittedly I didn't tell him that my con-dition was going to become chronic rather sooner than it had in my mother's case, while I was still in my thirties, but that was for a reason. A very good reason: I didn't know it myself.

When I was sixteen, standing in one of the school lavatories, I pissed blood. Later I learned that an abscess in one of my kidneys had burst, and that in years to come my kidneys would provide a home for many such.

Once the shock of the event had passed, I was actu-ally rather smug about it. In the fog of puberty what we were all looking for, my friends and I, was ways to be different from each other, as long as they were also ways of being different from the children that, deep down inside, we feared we still were.

Most of us settled for claiming we had lost our virginity in the holidays just past, or at the weekend at a party where there were no parents for miles, or during morning break. I seem to remember that long blonde perfumed hairs, to be draped negligently on one's jacket collar in a way that invited comment, changed hands at a premium. But as it turned out, congenital illness would do just as well, as a stark marker of before and after, as entry into the world of sex. It had the great advantage that the school nurse would corroborate it.

The doctor I was sent to told me gravely that I shouldn't think of marrying or having a family. In a way I really didn't take in what he was saying, that he was telling me to accustom myself to a very limited span of life. Marriage and family weren't exactly my obsessions, and it seemed that I was being given permission to put them out of my mind, and not to think of them again. It was like being let off games, which also happened, naturally enough, much to the envy of my schoolmates, without my having to ask for it or get piddling little notes week by week. I was Off Games wholesale and forever.

I suppose everyone who had power in my life, from the doctor who excused me from marriage and family on, was awkward and felt sorry for me – that was the distorting thing. Suddenly everyone was sorry for me. Everyone's reactions were falsified by pity, but since it happened at the same time with everybody I didn't really notice until it stopped. I resented it only when I looked back on that long period, those many years invalidated by pity.

My mother felt sorry for me, and guilty about the bodily legacy she was powerless to reverse. I suppose she had been holding her breath, in a way, all those years when it seemed that I had escaped my inheritance, and now the breath was knocked out of her in a sigh that had waited sixteen years to happen.

It was her liver killed her in the end. Hepatitis was something her system couldn't handle on top of everything else. But even then she wasn't thinking of her liver or her kidneys but of *my* kidneys, and strangely enough of my eyes. She didn't want me to see her in her bloatedness, and she always made sure the sheet was pulled up to her neck, her face made up, when I visited. She liked me to hold her hand, but she didn't want me to come too close. She wasn't being vain, it was just that everything she was going through was something I had to look forward to, and she thought that of the two of us she was actually the lucky one, because she was going through it for the first and only time. For her at least there had been no rehearsal, no anticipation.

When I told my parents I wanted to go to drama school – this was before my mother's liver joined her kidneys in their wildcat strike – I had expected opposition. In a way I think I wanted to be talked out of it, told that I was clever enough to go to university. But guilt had displaced all the natal signs on my parents' horoscopes, Leo and Virgo blotted out by We're-so-sorry, and they caved in right away. They thought that I was entitled to anything I wanted to do, in the time I had left to me.

After my mother died, my father's chief thought was paying off the mortgage on the house, so that it would come to me clean and unencumbered. One less thing to worry about. He managed it too, but he hadn't anticipated the M25, which was probably already drawn in dotted outline on maps that hung on walls in planning offices, even though it was years before anything was built. Built or pulled down. Dad would have hated the M25. He hated London already, he thought it was the opposite of a place, and he would have thought the M25 was another huge non-place, a non-place that obliterated perfectly decent real places in the interests of the non-place London.

I didn't anticipate the M25 either, or I would have sold the house before it was blighted, instead of renting it out. It was too near the M25-to-be, but not near enough. Blight is like nuclear war, if you're going to suffer anyway it's best to be at the point of impact: the Ground Zero of compulsory purchase rather than the large area financially poisoned by fall-out, where house prices never grow again.

Even at drama school, I suppose I was pitied. I remember one improv session in particular. In my memory we cleared the chairs away, to have room to express ourselves freely, but of course that can't be right. That period was actually a time without chairs, as if all the chairs had been collected and melted down, like park railings in an old-fashioned war. We all of us always sat on the floor, students and teachers alike, even older people who lowered themselves stiffly to the ground. Anyway, at this improv session our theme was fear, and I started talking about kidneys and what they had done to my mother, what they were likely in due course to do to me. I remember looking down at my sleeve – it was a paisley sleeve, if I'm absolutely honest – and seeing that I was plucking at it with my other hand. I thought, how interesting, people really do that in a crisis, I can use that. I can use that in my work.

I really made an impression. It was the high point of my drama school career. Then the student next to me stood up to do his improv. He had green eyes and wore a black polo-neck. He bit his nails down so far that I noticed they sometimes became infected. He would often have a fingertip bandaged, sometimes more than one, which didn't stop him from gnawing at them with his restless little teeth.

He put his hands behind his back and he never moved them after that. He kept his eyes cast down. He talked about having bone cancer in remission, about never knowing when the hand he trusted to pick up a teacup would let him down, and his voice sounded flat and uninvolved all the way through. And of course I was horrified. He made my 'fear' seem so remote, so self-indulgent, compared to what he went through every day.

We fetched up at the same pub at lunch-time. I don't

know about him, but I was quite shocked that there were still chairs in pubs. I was used by then to dinner parties where we sat around on cushions, balancing our plates of something-like-moussaka or fried cream. I even remember a tea-party where we all sat cross-legged on a waterbed. Although we sipped our tea gingerly and in unison, we were rocked by queasy tides. Our slightest movements, passing the sugar bowl, stirring our cups, even swallowing out of time, were unpredictably amplified, and every gesture left a sloshing wake of instability.

Now I think about it, the tea-party may not have been a social occasion at all, but an acting exercise designed to instil a sense of ensemble. To appear on stage is always like standing on a waterbed – that may have been the underlying idea. Trigorin yawning, Cordelia invisibly flinching, are linked to the other characters by bands of strong elastic, hydraulics of sympathy and antagonism. Nothing affects one person only, as we proved when we circulated plates fraught with scones. The liquid plinth beneath us dipped and rippled, and the tea sloshed unstoppably into our saucers.

So many things I did those days, in class and out of it, turned out to be acting exercises. I felt naïve in sophisticated company, and now in the pub with the incongruous chairs I felt embarrassed to have exposed my gauche fears in the presence of someone who was staring death in the face. I offered to buy him a drink.

I was flattered that he accepted. I was daring enough to ask how long he'd been in remission. 'Don't ask me,' he murmured into his pint. 'I had to say I was in remission, didn't I?' My throat tightened inside my (tell the truth) paisley foulard. I thought, This man is even braver than I thought. We were harrowed this morning, and still he was sparing us the full horror of his fate. I was about to ask, 'How long have you got?' but that seemed an unbearably crass thing to say.

Then he went on, 'I hadn't done any homework, so I had to say I was in remission, otherwise I'd have had to come up with some symptoms, wouldn't I? Anyway, you'd been pretty fancy, so I had to strip right down. I think it worked.' He looked at me suspiciously. 'Were you tipped off about today's theme? Are you teacher's pet or something? How do you know so much about poly-whatsit kidney disease?' And of course I stood there like a fool and I said, 'Because I suffer from it. Because it's true.'

And he smiled a crooked smile as if he'd caught me cheating in some way. Which he had. Already that day I had an inkling that one of us would be getting a lot of work, and that it wasn't going to be me. It was going to be him. You can often see him on TV even now. His eyes are green. He's stopped biting his nails.

Of course I was the green-eyed one, when I realized that his lie beat my truth at its own game. But he did me a favour really, by making me face the fact that I'd been coasting for far too long, on a hard-luck story that hadn't even happened yet.

I'd never thought of myself as somebody with an illness, but after that fateful day of improv I learned not to think of myself as someone who was even living in the shadow of an illness, except when the anniversary of my mother's death came around.

When I started up with Terry, I told him about my kidneys, but I didn't make a song and dance about it. My kidneys were only part of that dowry of damage any two people bring to each other when they set up as a couple. They claimed no great attention, early on.

But it's a different story when you're crawling through the day on your hands and knees, when you seem to be living uphill and the slope gets a fraction steeper every day. It's a different story when your BUN – that's Blood Urea Nitrogen – is up to 233. They put me on dialysis right away, and they told me mine was the highest reading they had ever seen. Yours, if it's normal, is under 20. Of course yours is normal.

Kidney disease is a bore. I wish I could tell you different. You spend four hours hooked up to a machine three times a week, with no one more interesting to talk to than a nurse. Maybe renal units attract a particularly dour class of nurse for some reason. There aren't a lot of laughs on a renal unit. The Bumper Book of Kidney Jokes would fit comfortably into your back pocket. Here's one: *I used to think the Fistula was a river in Poland until I discovered dialysis.* That's renal humour for you. In fact that's a classic moment in the history of renal humour – something of a milestone.

Kids these days, with their Gore-Tex grafts and their high-flux machines. Two hours for dialysis! That's not kidney failure. That's a holiday.

A fistula is a sort of artificial super bloodvessel they make by putting together two of your regular ones, to speed up dialysis. You can put your finger on the fistula while you're on dialysis and feel it thrumming with all the extra work it's doing. It's a strange sensation.

The technical term for the trembling that a fistula makes is 'thrilling', but I really resent the word. There's all the difference in the world between the humour that comes from the patient and the humour that comes from the doctors and nurses. It really gets on my tits when the trained staff start having their bit of fun. They check that the fistula is functioning properly before they start the dialysis, and someone's sure to ask, oh so deadpan, 'Is it thrilling?', just waiting for the witty reply, 'It's a thrill a minute.' Only it's not, it's a foreign body in *my* body and it's humming like a transformer that's about to blow up. Jokes about 'thrilling' aren't renal humour, they're jokes around you, jokes about you, cheap disinfectant, cheap anaesthetic.

Kidney disease is a full-time job, more or less, so it was handy that I could make my living in a few hours a week. In the world of voice-over actors there are the stars, people who are paid to sound like themselves, and foot-soldiers like me. I think we have much the easier job, we nobodies, though we also have the harder job getting established. We only get known for doing the job by doing the job.

I remember when all my work was on ads that got broadcast late at night in the regions, in the provinces of the country and also the clock. The first time I had an ad on prime time in the south-east – an ad my friends might see, whether they recognized the voice or not – it felt the way I imagine it must feel to be acting in the West End after years of dismal rep.

It's different for the stars, who bring their glorious voices to market rather more anxiously, the poor darlings. The stars and their agents are always having to make calculations of what is lost and what is gained by lending their vocal prestige to a product. They measure out the integrity-molecules for cash. For example: my recent appearance as a sad Victorian in a classy television series allows me to ask for x more than last time, but does it mean that endorsing nostalgic cakes is now beneath me? Does my smashing success as a mad killer in a Hollywood shocker make it ridiculous that I am now recommending life insurance?

I never had to bother with anything like that. Somehow my job never required me to sound like myself. In fact by some perverse logic the most convincing ads I did, from a vocal point of view, involved changing my natural pitch or tempo – going very basso for men's toiletries, of course, speaking very bouncily and fast for anything colourful or slimming – and doing unearthly things with consonants. I was able to find the right confiding tones for 'Dogs instinctively know what they like, and what's good for them' in one take.

Technically, it's a difficult line – who do they get to make these things up? – because it combines two quite different sorts of nonsense, and you have to watch yourself near the comma, where the nonsense changes gear. 'Dogs instinctively know what they like.' Try saying that aloud without thinking. Of course they do. *Everything* instinctively knows what it likes. That's no more than a clumsy definition of instinct. A great white shark knows what it likes. A virus – the common cold knows what it likes. That's how these organisms go on being alive. Now try saying 'and what's good for them', without thinking (which will certainly show up in your voice) of course they *don't*. If they did, they wouldn't be dogs. They'd be dietitians or philosophers. It's tricky, I don't deny it. But I managed it in one take.

There was only one line that ever really baffled my technique. It was in an ad for a deodorizing insole, and I played The Man Who's Afraid His Feet Smell. He and his date stroll into a restaurant. The development of the little drama makes it clear that this is a time of first impressions and huge male worry. Looking around her, she exclaims, 'Authentic Japanese! Let's take our shoes off!' Innocently she plunges her companion into social hell. His cheese secrets are about to be broadcast to the world. He thinks fast. He says, 'Let's eat Italian!'

Let's eat Italian. Not much of a challenge, you'd think, to a voice artist with my experience, and still I couldn't do it. It had to do with the filmed part of the advert looking so old. The fashions were so dated they were like a costume history exhibit, from the Naff Wing of the Bad Taste Museum. Obviously these cheese-absorbing insoles were a venerable product in America, and the British distributors were lazily redubbing old advertising footage with an English accent. Not a lot was being asked of me, in a sense. Just a new voice-track to go with old images. But British voices come out of British bodies – I hope that doesn't sound too Method-actor-temperamental – and I couldn't get a plausible sound, to go with the boxy American body in the advert, that didn't actually sound American. Everything I did sounded jarring. We didn't give up, and I kept on trying. Normally of course I do true voice-overs, where there's no body to correspond to the voice, just an implied speaker with an authority that doesn't need to be earned. But that wasn't the deepest reason for my making such heavy weather of the Fragrasole advert.

For some people, a tantalus can be a dog's water bowl, standing next to a saucer of crusted offal. This I know. For some people, a tantalus can be a dripping tap, even if it's only a sound effect in a radio play.

My mouth was dry. My mouth was on the farthest shore of dryness. There was no moisture available anywhere in my system to lubricate the vocal instrument. I had a glass of water, of course, next to the microphone, but I couldn't touch it. Dialysis is bossy. Dialysis tells you what you can and can't do. I was like a hen-pecked husband, married to a machine that owed me no loyalty in return. I wasn't allowed anything that would make me thirsty, and I wasn't allowed anything that would give my pathetic kidneys more than the bare minimum to do, between sessions on the machine. In other words: nothing salty, nothing alcoholic. No bacon, no Beaujolais.

You make all sorts of surprising discoveries, dull surprising discoveries, when you're married to the machine, like that having less than an ounce of cheese is worse than having no cheese at all. It's easy to split the cheese atom. If you restrict yourself to a smudge of cheese in a day, you have no sense of being in the presence of cheese, somehow, and it's better to give up on it altogether.

You have to become a boring sort of food analyst, scanning the plates for the potassium your body can't tolerate. There are innocent-seeming foodstuffs that carry depth-charges of potassium: potatoes, bananas, instant coffee. Well, there's nothing innocent about instant coffee. You can never have too many reasons for refusing instant coffee. And potatoes and bananas have never been staples of *haute cuisine* down our way. Not many hosts serve chips as a main course in my social circle, and not many hosts come through from the kitchen with their cheeks pride-flushed to announce, 'Guess what you're having for afters, you lucky people. *Narnibars!*' And of course if you say no to a helping of potatoes, there's always someone who says, 'You *are* good,' while they let their plates be piled high.

No one ever said 'You *are* good' when I put my hand over my water glass to stop it being refilled, but that was my real martyrdom. I was restricted to a total liquid intake of a pint and a quarter a day. No soup, obviously, unless I measured it and had it count towards my total.

It was still relatively early, on the day that I dried on 'Let's eat Italian,' dried and stayed dry, and I had already been through sixteen of my permitted twenty-five fluid ounces. I didn't dare drink any more. I was already tetchy enough in the evenings with Terry, just because his body allowed him a nightcap, a glass of wine or a whisky, and mine didn't.

I could have broken the rules, of course. I always had that option, but it would have done me no good in the long run. The dialysis machine calls the shots, in a strange way. It's a stroppy servant, ordering its masters about. It demands co-operation, even gratitude for the grudging scrub it gives your bloodstream. It demands unselfishness. It's not fair on the others – that's the line it takes – the other users of the machine, if you take more than your rightful share of dialysis. The dialysis cake is cut into equal slivers, and those who ask for more shall get nothing, not a crumb. I was always aware of the people waiting in the queue for dialysis, who would be happy to take my place in no time flat, if I was stupid enough to test the machine's patience.

It's funny, but I never doubted that the machine would know if I cheated. In my mind if nowhere else, the lifesaver was also a lie detector. The dialysis machine doubled as a polygraph, and I had to be truthful. I had to leave the water glass alone, even when my throat was as dry as the driest thing there is. As dry as a deodorizing insole.

The actress who was playing my date had already recorded her contribution to everyone's satisfaction, but she was kind enough to help me out by repeating her line take after take, in the hope of bringing a little spontaneity to my performance. It was humiliating. I have never been so humiliated. Time after time she'd cry, 'Authentic Japanese!' with a convincing slim freshness, though she was a lunch addict of considerable size, largely composed of junk food by the look of her. Take after take she'd exclaim, 'Let's take our shoes off!', pitching the line exactly as it should be pitched, between innocence and worldliness, old enough to have no fear of exotic cuisine, young enough to regard it, still, as an adventure. And every time I'd give my line a reading that was as dry and flat and bland as high street pizza.

Eventually she gave up and left. Things were getting desperate. The producer kept giving me the green light, but I couldn't get my voice into gear. For the first time in my working life I could feel confidence leaking away through the glass. If I didn't come up with something soon, they'd hire a replacement. They'd have to. I closed my eyes and concentrated.

I stopped thinking about The Man Who's Afraid His Feet Smell, about his silly clothes, about the sort of sound his body would make when it spoke. I thought only of Italian food, not the commercialized crap that the couple in the advert would shovel down in whatever eatery took their fancy, but the real thing. Pungent sauces, strong flavours, grouse in Barolo, risottos tinted with ink, Tuscan hare sauce for pappardelle. I like game but I don't care for offal, tripe and brains, heart and lungs, liver and kidneys. My sense of irony isn't as highly developed as all that. That's rather a lot to hope for. But that was my only limit. Mentally, I set myself to slavering over any Italian food, no matter how elaborate or homely – humble polenta, say, that you have to stir and stir until your elbows ache with it, but sets in the end into a delicious bland golden brick of friable starch.

I concentrated on the moist look of food in cookery photographs, the burnish, the gloss, the visual promises of deliciousness. I turned it into a magic spell, a mantra: the *sheen* of *cuisine*, the *sheen* of *cuisine*.

Then finally my glands responded, as I sat there with my eyes closed, and the waters of hunger came at last to refresh my mouth. It was a sudden appearance of healing moisture, long despaired of by my throat, like an access of tears.

After that I was able to do it, somehow. Perhaps all I needed all along had been that extra bit of imaginative saliva in my reading of the line.

Given my fluctuating energy level, it was handy that I not only had a job that was effectively part time, but a hobby that didn't take me out of the house. If the Peter Hunter part of my life had been devoted to bird-watching, say, or bell-ringing, my manky kidneys would have bent my life out of shape years before they did.

What I'd said to Vicar Bob, that Terry and I didn't sleep together, wasn't 100 per cent true. Sometimes in early days Terry would spend the night in my bed, until my tossing and turning drove him reluctantly back to his own. After I went on to dialysis, that was no longer possible. Even sleeping alone, I would sometimes lie on my arm, and of course the chances of that happening were much greater if I shared the bed. Lying on your arm is a thoroughly bad idea, but of course you don't know that when you're asleep. That's the whole point of being asleep, the not knowing good from bad. Anyway, if my arm got slept on, I would be likely to get an aneurysm in my fistula, and take it from me, if there's one thing you don't want in your fistula, it's an aneurysm. And if there's one place you don't want an aneurysm, it's your fistula.

A fistula's a bit of a liability at the best of times. It's not natural, is it? It's no more than a shotgun wedding between a vein and an artery. Of course that's the great thing about a fistula, its not being natural, if it happens to be your body's nature to let you down as badly as mine had. But over time a fistula tends to harden up, to become sclerotic, and then they have to start again somewhere else. After a few years, I had these odd purple calcified curves on the inner aspect of my arm. It looked as if I had those hard curved pasta tubes that American cookbooks call 'elbows' inserted under the skin, every few inches, in an almost decorative pattern. Very pretty.

By that time I didn't have much of an appetite, but I always cooked for Terry as if I was trying to impress him on a first date. It's going a bit far to say that I was like Beethoven in his deafness, creating harmonies that I could no longer physically appreciate, but I was certainly trying to meet standards that no longer meant anything much to me directly. Terry sometimes told me I shouldn't try so hard, that I had nothing to prove, but it was stronger than me. Love is never satisfied with the proofs it has furnished, and my heart was borne towards Terry on a strong current of catering.

Love is not a convenience food. Love is not instant, freeze-dried or microwave compatible. A cramped kitchen, lack of equipment: these are challenges, they can never be excuses. With tinned soup there is no love. With frozen pastry there is no love. Stock cubes likewise are the death of love.

Besides which, it made sense for me to play host, whenever I felt up to it, rather than be guest in other people's houses, which called for much more mental discipline, to the point where it was no longer possible for me even to pretend I was enjoying myself. My dialysis schedule (sessions on Monday, Wednesday and Friday morning) ruled over everything. So if it was a Monday, Wednesday or Friday evening, then I could allow myself to eat salted food, knowing that if need be I could go over the pint-and-a-quarter limit and compensate with extra self-restraint the next day. But that way I would always end up by taking it out on Terry. At least on Tuesday or Thursday night I knew there was no possible leeway, but I never did learn the knack of leaving food on my plate without feeling I was giving offence, and I didn't want to bore people with the fascinating story of my renal breakdown and the rules it made for my life. I didn't want to become one of those people who aren't happy till they've turned the conversation round to themselves. Illness can do that to you, if you don't watch out. Sometimes when I laid my knife and fork together prematurely, I would find myself suppressing a sigh, as if deep down I wanted nothing better than to tell the company what I was going through.

Saturday was a special case, since in theory I had a full day to go before my next dialysis, so I could have swigged a bit and gone short on Sunday. I could have opened my mouth and taken a deep breath of the water I needed so badly. But I only tried that once. Sunday was grim enough without me inventing hardships for myself.

I don't know for a fact that people with kidney disease have a smell to them, a smell that gets worse as the days pass between sessions of dialysis. People with liver disease certainly do – the pungent metallic smell of my Mum in her last illness – and liver and kidneys are both in the purifying business, so it seems logical. But I don't know it for a fact. Your nose has better things to do than keep you informed about your personal freshness (I've been paid good money as a voice-over artist to play on people's fears in this exact area). And it wasn't something I felt able to ask Terry. *Do I suffer from a stink cycle, darling, on top of all my other attractions?* I preferred to remain in the dark. But if I did have a smell to me – and I'm not saying I did – but if I did, then Sunday evening was when it was at its worst, such a long time after Friday's dialysis, and it made sense to steer clear of company.

As eating became a more complicated pleasure, and then stopped being a pleasure at all, entertaining became more and more important. Illness takes you out of your world, if you let it, and I wasn't going to let go of my world so easily. It grieved me to cook without salt, and to leave my guests to season their food at table individually. It felt uncivilized. But more than that, the two tastes are quite different, cooked salt and raw. Raw salt is brash and unsubtle; it has had no chance to permeate a dish. I felt I was shortchanging our guests by offering only the crudest form of seasoning, as if I didn't know any better.

Successful entertaining is never spontaneous, everybody knows that, but often it felt as if I was having to stylize my reactions to a really ridiculous extent. I would try to play the open-handed host while actually linking my thumbs behind my chair, to keep my hands from forgetting themselves. Even so, all it would take would be one airy gesture, one moment of letting my guard down – laughing at a joke, enjoying a story – and I would find my hands being magnetized towards a glass that I dared not refill with the water that my thirst demanded. Meanwhile I would be watching my guests' glasses, ready to top them up with wine while also keeping their water glasses brimming.

Just by sitting sociably at my table, guests seemed to be advertising the purifying powers of their kidneys. Look at me, they seemed to be saying, I can drink water, and not even count the ounces. That's nothing, someone else would seem to be saying, *I'm* drinking wine – red wine at that! – and after dinner I think I'll treat myself to a brandy, if I'm offered.

Of course he was offered. He was a guest.

They were so silently smug, though, about their bodies' talent for eliminating poison. It was as if they were saying ever so casually, oh yes, I can eat broken glass, can't everybody? There's nothing I like better for breakfast than a bowl of razor blades, and then I wash it down with brake fluid, glass after glass of the stuff. My kidneys just lap it all up. They come back asking for more.

The stupid thing was that every time I tipped a bottle over a guest's glass, every time the wine gurgled through the bottle's neck and splashed decorously into the waiting curve of the glass, my parched mouth prepared itself by futile reflex to drink. My tongue bathed itself in fool's saliva. Then I would sit down again, smiling all the while, and reach my hands behind my chair to lock my thumbs against temptation.

Sometimes our guests, quite innocently, would have me pulling at my thumbs in a deadlocked tug-of-war, until I thought that the thumb joints would snap or my elbows dislocate. There was a Harley Street doctor in the news at one time, who had been buying kidneys in Turkey – that is, paying people a few pounds to have one kidney taken out – and putting them into his private patients. And after dessert everybody round the table, round *my* table, was sounding off about how shocking this was. At first I thought I was going to be satisfied with being ironical, the wry host, not upsetting anyone, just making a point, and I said, 'Heavens, what a terrible thing! And you say that what this doctor has been doing may not even be illegal, unprofessional yes, but not illegal?' My eyebrows waggled so much that I thought they might go into spasm. 'Of course it raises any number of ethical problems, profoundly troubling questions. I don't suppose anybody remembers the doctor's name and address, do they? Phone number, anyone?'

But then I found that my thumbs had given each other the slip. They had sneaked past each other, and I found that I was more or less pounding the table, with a force that made all the glasses shake. Every single crystal tantalus shook. 'Let's put our cards on the table, shall we?' I said, and then I realized I wasn't being altogether clear, that it sounded like a figure of speech and not a specific challenge. 'I mean it,' I said. 'Let's all put our donor cards on the table. That way we'll know who's really concerned, and who's just sounding off for the sake of hearing their own voice.' Terry winced, and exercised the host's privilege of beating a retreat to the kitchen and closing the door behind him.

One or two of our guests had the grace to look sheepish, and I could hear the muffled tactful impact of lover's heel on lover's shin as people realized they'd been thoughtless. But one of our guests, a workmate of Terry's who I didn't know particularly well, wasn't at all abashed. He said, 'I used to carry a donor card, but last year I tore it up.'

It was a sentence I never thought I'd hear. It took my breath away. Instantly it cleared a space that was too huge for me to fill right off, with protests that took a little time to formulate. It was like someone saying,

Once upon a time I wanted to save your life. But then I thought better of it.

This man was wearing a T-shirt with the slogan *Fashion cares* . . . In my grandparents' day and even to some extent in my parents', it was thought rude to discuss politics at a social occasion. I'm not so stuffy, but I do think you shouldn't go out to dinner dressed as a slogan unless the invitation specifically asks you to. What kind of person wears a T-shirt to a dinner party anyway? It's possible – I'm being very fair here – that the T-shirt wasn't quite as smug as it looked. It's possible that the slogan was in two parts, so that the back panel of the T-shirt might say . . . *but only after a fashion*, or something of that sort, but that would only be a different kind of smugness, the smugness of imagining that you're worth more than one look. That your upper body will be stared at coming and going.

I had to start my protest. I had to start filling the great space that had opened up. I cleared my dry throat as best I could. I said, 'Why on earth did you do that?'

He didn't seem in the least embarrassed. He seemed to have no difficulty in meeting my eyes. 'Well, it stands to reason that all of us here are in a high-risk group for Aids.' He made a sort of gesture of spreading his hands outwards, as if he was appealing for support but was actually very sure of getting it, as if everybody at the table except me had a true sense of priorities. 'So where's the sense in donating organs that can infect the people you're trying to help?'

I hadn't thought through exactly what my reaction

was, but I wasn't going to let the matter drop. 'Sorry if this is none of my business, but you've made it my business, our business, do you mind telling us if you've actually taken the Test?'

He lit a cigarette. He had already filled an ashtray with long stubs. Smoking's bad enough when it's done well, but I do hate *sippy* smokers, smokers who take a few rushed puffs and then stub out a butt that's only half burned down. Even when they're not at work, it's as if they're scared to death of a supervisor coming along and telling them off.

Gay people shouldn't smoke, anyway. It's dangerous. A cigarette extends beyond the hand what, four inches at most, and yet that little extension can be fatal. It's something you learn in drama school, that a cigarette is a difficult and demanding prop, on stage or off, and not for beginners. When the slightest wave of the hand has a follow-spot of accentuating smoke, body language becomes theatrical. Even manly gestures nellify. This dinner guest of mine, flapping his hands to waft away smoke as if it was someone else who was making it drift across his face, threw away with every flap the virtues of his firm chin, his practised smoking-or-non-smoking-sir smile.

Terry's friend (our guest, but Terry's friend) didn't look away from my – I suppose – rather aggressive glare, my aggressive question. 'No, I don't mind at all,' he said at last. 'No, I haven't taken the Test.'

I was aware at that moment that I was crossing a boundary of some sort between civilized and uncivilized behaviour, but by this time I couldn't stop myself. 'And would you mind telling us why not, if you're so concerned about what happens to other people? Wouldn't it be more responsible to take the Test and know for sure, before you tear up your little red card?'

At least that got some sort of reaction from him. He made a gesture that was like a priest crossing himself, only he stopped it in the middle, with his right finger touching his left shoulder. His finger rested on a little loop of red ribbon, not a rosette or anything elaborate like that, but just a few inches folded over and fastened with a pin. I hadn't noticed it before, or if I had I'd thought it was only part of the design of his imbecile T-shirt. But now I saw that it was an actual piece of ribbon, and he was resting a finger on it. Perhaps he was trying to start a fashion, a craze for the unilateral epaulette.

'You don't know what you're asking,' he said.

If he hadn't had his legs under my table and my food in his belly, not to mention the socially administered poisons already being broken down by competent kidneys, he might have added, 'Where have you been all this time?' I'd been at home, mostly, nursing my strength, tending my lover. I'd been under the house arrest imposed by my condition. Inertia with outings.

I'm sorry to say that I might have pressed the point even then, if I'd been able to come up with a satisfactory way of voicing my bitterness. Clearly it isn't an enviable position, not knowing whether you're going to get sick or not, but from where I was sitting, entrenched in the presence of renal failure, I can only say that it seemed so. Knowledge oppressing those who know; uncertainty crushing to the uncertain. Over the years I'd got used to people who didn't want to drink alcohol bringing bottles of mineral water with them to dinner parties, as if I – of all people! – might be unprepared for the trauma of teetotalism. But this guest had gone one further. It was as if he had brought his own air with him in a bottle. We who sat at the same table and had tasted the same food, host and guest, somehow didn't breathe the same atmosphere.

Then Terry came in from the kitchen with silent fireworks on a tray, bearing what looked like egg-cups of soft flame. He had been busy out there, at a time of what must have seemed social crisis. He had done what he could with a desperate calm, probably thinking it was too late to make any difference. The disaster had happened already, but he pressed grimly on, like someone whitewashing the windows after the four-minute warning, reading the civil defence manual by the purple light of apocalypse.

He had done what he could, while the world ended in the dining-room. He had dug out a bottle of grappa from a cupboard, warmed it frantically in a pan and poured it into liqueur glasses. Just before he came back into the dining-room he had lit a match with a trembling hand and held it above each glass in turn.

On the tray that Terry brought in was a little phalanx of flames, blue wavering cones giving each glass an impalpable lid of ignited vapour. Deep down I have the feeling that *flambé*ing food or drink is pretentious (not when you flame a dish for a specific purpose during cooking, of course), but I suppose that's what Terry was counting on, the ooh-ah factor, the showmanship of drinkable fire. Certainly someone dashed across the room to turn some of the lights off, so that we could better appreciate the display. It may even have been the lover of the donor-card vandal – the revoker of promises, miser of organs – freed by Terry's tact from social deadlock.

I let my thimble of grappa burn and burn, long after everyone else had blown the flames out and raised their glasses tentatively to their lips. It was only a courtesy that Terry had poured me a glass. I couldn't drink it, obviously, but he wanted to spare me the embarrassment of looking excluded. My thumbs found each other again, behind my chair, as I watched the flame on top of the liquid die slowly down as the alcohol was consumed. It had a symbolic look about it, the tempting drink under its taboo of fire, but I can't say it was a particular deprivation keeping my hands off it. Nobody actually likes grappa very much, which is why there is always some hanging around in kitchen cupboards, long after everything else in the house has been drunk.

Perhaps – this is a new thought – the man with the red ribbon on his shoulder really didn't know about my condition. Perhaps he wasn't being as crass as I assumed. I tried not to be boring about my medical history, and I didn't bring the subject up unless somebody asked, but at the same time I took it for granted that everybody knew, through Terry. But Terry wasn't a press agent, and he probably felt as awkward as I did about putting people in the picture. So perhaps there were people around my table who really didn't know. How odd to think of that now.

I have to admit I was wrong about something else. The red ribbon-loop did actually take off in a small way as a fashion accessory, so perhaps Terry's social circle were closer to being trend-setters than I ever thought possible. Of course, most people had the sense to wear it with something dressier than a T-shirt. I even seem to remember seeing film stars making Oscar acceptance speeches, with a little scarlet accent pinned to their shining-dark lapels.

The night of my outburst, of anguish and tact and grappa, was a Saturday night. The next day I had to go through the non-drinker's hangover that is a dialysis patient's Sunday, and the day after that was my next appointment with the machine.

The renal unit was about fifteen miles away. I would drive there exhausted and drive back sore but manic. On my way there, one day, in the car, I saw a little convoy of learner motor cyclists. They were wearing neon tabards with the inscription LEARNER UNDER INSTRUCTION, and they were playing a ragged game of follow-my-leader behind the instructor, like ducklings behind their mother or, I suppose, behind any creature that has imprinted its image on their tiny minds.

Every now and then the instructor would look over his shoulder, and the fledgling bikers would repeat the gesture rather desperately, wobbling and weaving on their unfamiliar wheels.

My old Dad used to shake his head, when the ton-up boys came roaring down the road past the house, and say that what they really were was murder-cycles. Bikes never had any mystique for me, I have to say, despite this dreadful warning. The only machines I've looked at with any attention have been the ones that Peter Hunter has mounted or been mounted on, the various machines that he has had his magnificent haunches astride, or been brusquely bent over, in the course of his image-making career. Once in 1983, I remember, he paid the chrome-and-glass speedometer binnacle of a classic bike (a British model, even, if memory serves) an eerie homage with the very tip of his tongue. That haunting tongue, so often submissive, never humble. But seeing the fragile convoy of learner bikers, I started taking a new interest. It stood to reason that I was looking at the most likely source of my replacement kidney, if I was lucky enough to get the chance of such a thing.

When the subject first came up, Terry hadn't known what his blood group was, only that it was nothing special, and until he found out, there was a possibility of love requiring a kidney from him. Even if we'd shared a blood type, there was no guarantee of donor compatibility, but it was a first step. I know he was disappointed when it turned out he was O and not A, but we both knew he was also relieved.

The hardest thing he ever had to do in his career was getting all the jabs he needed for international travel, and donating a kidney would be an altogether tougher test of squeamishness. We did talk about him becoming a donor anyway, for someone else, someone who could use his kidney, but his heart wasn't in it, and I can't say I was surprised. Terry couldn't be a part of a utopian exchange. He wouldn't have the courage to cast a kidney upon the waters, hoping to have it come back not multiplied, or however the phrase goes, but with its blood type adjusted for my convenience.

The next time I had a few hours free in town, after a job, I went to Her Majesty's Stationery Office and bought the police handbook – better than that, the Police Method – of motor-cycle riding. The assistants at HMSO were perfectly polite when I told them what I was after, but something about their manner made me think they saw right through me. They knew I wasn't the biker type. Perhaps they guessed what my interest really was.

I didn't want Terry seeing the HMSO bag, in case he asked what was in it, but I could hardly wave around a motor-cycling handbook without some sort of explanation. So I paid a visit to the Elizabeth David shop, and bought a gravy boat I didn't need. That way I could secrete the book safely in a bag that gave nothing away.

I kept the book in a bedside drawer, and it became my bedtime reading for a while. It kept me company in the watches of the night. In some ways it was rather an inspiring read, for someone with my admittedly special-ized point of view. I mean, every vehicle is a potential accident, I realize that, but motor cyclists really are organ donors-in-waiting. A dab of grease or a handful of gravel, and a motor bike just wants a good lie down.

Bikers have two sets of brakes, for instance, which they need to apply differently in different circumstances: the foot brake controlling the rear wheel, the hand brake – mounted on the right handlebar – controlling the front. It's not safe to apply the hand brake on a corner. On the straight, you should apply the front brake about a second before the rear brake in proportional pressures of 75 per cent to 25 per cent. In wet weather, both together and with equal force. Got that? Nor had most of the bikers I watched. I became a little obsessive in my watching of bikers. From what I could see – and I have to say my heart leaped – most bikers didn't use the foot brake at all, even in wet weather or on corners. Not even on corners in wet weather.

As time went by, I found my eyes were drawn to the rear contour of bikers' leather jackets. The handbook recommended wearing a jacket with an extra panel of padding near waist level. It was for kidney protection. My immediate reaction was, oh yes, protect those kidneys. We don't want anything to happen to *them*. I read that the panel protects not only against injury, but against the long-term effects of cold, which can lead to recurrent infections. Kidney fitness is important.

I read in the handbook that most motor-cycle accidents are caused by motorists turning right without indicating. The motor cyclist, riding serenely on the outside of the traffic, encounters a sudden wall of metal. That smooth wall will make things rough for him. After

I read that, I had to take particular care with that manoeuvre. It wasn't that I'd ever been negligent in those circumstances, so far as I knew, and I wasn't about to commit a murder. But I was tempted, really tempted, not to signal, not to look in my mirrors, and just leave it to chance. It all came down to chance in the end.

Even after I'd consciously decided against negligence, I was afraid that unless I made a point of it and was actively vigilant, I might end up doing it 'without meaning to', the way I used to slurp a lot of tomato ketchup on to my plate, when I was a kid, accidentally on purpose. That wouldn't be very clever, deep down. I could see it wouldn't be kosher to do your own culling, to splash the road metal with tomato sauce accidentally on purpose. But still I needed that kidney.

There were rules, you see, about transplant eligibility. Beyond a certain age you weren't in the running. And every antibody you had in your bloodstream brought you nearer to the point of being a bad risk, for a transplant and all its complications. I couldn't wait forever.

But as time went on, and I learned more about the subject, it seemed that every bit of good news was cancelled out by a bit of bad. For instance. Bikers are supposed to do three 'observations' – actual turns of the head – for every time they take a turning or make a manoeuvre, since bike mirrors, apparently, don't give a complete picture of what's behind them. Once before signalling, to make sure there is enough room behind them to allow embarking on the intended manoeuvre; a second time, to make sure the message has been received and understood, that traffic is holding back or making room; and a third time – the 'lifesaver' – immediately before turning or changing lane. None of the bikers that I saw, that I watched, did anything of the sort. They couldn't care less about the lifesaver. They didn't give death even the fleeting backward glance that is required from everybody always.

That was all plus. On the minus side, bikers are legally obliged to wear helmets, and many of them choose to put their headlights on in the day, to make sure of being seen.

On the other hand, passers-by finding injured bikers tend to take their helmets off, which isn't at all a good idea. It can easily undo all the good the helmet has done in the crash itself. I've even seen bikers – before they roar off from the lights – with DO NOT REMOVE stickers attached to their helmets. But who reads stickers in an emergency? Act fast. No time to lose. Take his helmet off, quick! Click click oh dear.

Oh dear. May as well dig out his kidney, now. There, behind the protective panel.

One of the things I learned from the handbook – it's common sense – was that bikers were supposed to go slower in the wet, what with their non-existent margin of error being plunged even further into the minus. It seemed to me, all the same, that it was business as usual in the wet. Once I even rolled down the car window and asked a courier rider who was waiting at the lights in a

downpour, racing his throttle like a true kidney kami-
kaze, why he drove just as fast whatever the weather.

Lashed to the carrying rack behind him was a soft toy
of some sort, some mascot, but its synthetic fur had
taken on so much water that you couldn't tell what
animal or character it was supposed to represent. Its
cuddly identity was quite drowned.

Why do you drive so fast in the wet? It just popped
into my head to ask the question, I hadn't rehearsed it. I
blinked my eyes against the rain that was being blown
in through the window I had opened. The biker's
answer, delivered with a grin, was perfectly straight-
forward, and I believed he gave me the true reason: *The
Old Bill doesn't book you in the rain. The Bill likes to keep his
uniform dry.* Simple words, yet they had the power to
make me happy.

Courier riders must be particularly vulnerable, since
not only do they have to work in all weathers, but
they're inevitably exceeding the concentration param-
eters recommended in the handbook. The handbook
says that an hour at a stretch is the longest you can
reasonably expect to maintain the vigilance necessary
for defensive riding.

Once I noticed that a courier rider waiting at the lights
had a sticker on his 'top box', saying I SUPPORT THE
AMBULANCE WORKERS – I MAY BE THEIR NEXT LOAD.
There was some sort of industrial action going on at the
time, I seem to remember.

This biker was wearing a full-faced helmet, as recommended by the handbook, but he had raised the visor a

little to allow for the insertion of a cigarette. He was smoking the cigarette at an upward angle which had less to do with jauntiness than with the limitations of helmet design. I'm no friend of smoking as a general thing, but for once I wouldn't think of contesting this boy's decision to abuse his body. He was on a do-or-die mission, like all his breed. He was allowed to take lesser risks without a nagging. I even felt that they should build cigarette-holders into the helmets themselves, to make smoking easier. These brave boys had a right to their cigarettes, to anything that kept them happy.

Except maybe the tape deck that he had on his machine, blaring out sound, which would be a whipping offence in any well-run world. He had to play his music pretty bloody loud, if it was to have any chance of getting through the helmet to his ears. At least he was stopped at the lights, so he wasn't setting up that Doppler effect which is so maddening for pedestrians. I even recognized the tune that he was playing.

It was full of a sort of nagging consolation, and it was called 'Song for Guy' by Elton John. Elton John's never earned a penny piece of royalties from me, I have to say, but Terry was quite a fan in a quiet sort of way. It was Terry who told me that 'Song for Guy' was a tribute to a motor-cycle courier who had been killed during the recording of a particular album. It's an instrumental track, but Terry liked the bit near the end where if you listen carefully you can hear Elton singing 'Life isn't everything' very quietly in the background. So that should have seemed like a good omen, a healthy premonition.

But I was in a rather extreme state of mind, for some reason. I kept looking at the sticker on the top box of the motor bike. He supported the ambulance workers. He might be their next load. It seemed actually cruel, the way he was flaunting the nearness of his kidneys. I felt I could almost smell those wet gadgets. I could almost hear the silent simmering of filtration.

There was a length of orange flex running from his belt-loop to the ignition key in its slot. This arrangement had the strange effect of making him look as if he was already on life support, the machine keeping him almost as a pet. I even had the feeling that if I was able to reach out of the car and switch the ignition off, not only would the engine stop turning, but so would everything that was keeping him alive. Heart spluttering to a standstill, he would slump across the handlebars. The bike itself would fall over unless I intervened, suddenly strong, to lay machine and rider gently on the ground. Then his kidneys would be mine for the asking.

There was another sticker on the back of his helmet, with the slogan *Think Bike!* I didn't need to be told. I thought Bike. I thought Biker.

Sitting next to him at the lights, I couldn't see the face that his helmet hid, but I could see the hawser of young hair that stuck down from the back of his helmet, caught in a pony-tail with a red rubber band. I could see the extra padded panel of his jacket that, in a crash, would offer protection that might turn out to be important. I could see the reinforced white plastic disc of his knee-pad, peeping through a tear in the leather from some occasion in the past when his body had dived unsuccessfully to disperse itself.

All along I knew the odds were against me. Did you know there is just one group of road-users whose casualties have declined steadily over the last five years? That's right. Motor cyclists. Isn't that just what you'd expect?

It's worse than that, even. Sales of motor cycles are down, across the board. It's mainly that so many get stolen, and the cost of insurance is getting astronomical. But the rise in insurance costs is discriminatory, that's what's so unfair. It's pricing the young and the reckless out of biking altogether, the hard-core donors, and then what's to become of me? Of course people with too much money go on buying fancy machines as a status symbol instead of a second car, but that's no use to me.

They keep their farty darlings in the garage if there's as much as a single grey cloud in the sky. They change the tyres every day, so that the tread has an eerie distinctness. Their tyres are so new you can see a virgin whisker of rubber at the centre of each pore-lozenge of tread. In a patch of mud their tyres would make a clear and absolutely unblurred impression, they would clench and clench and not give in to a skid, but of course these motor bikes never see mud. They don't know what mud is.

Their owners polish them more than they ride them, these machines so loaded with extras they seem more like thin cars than fat motor bikes. When they do deign to climb aboard the oiled and buffed saddle with its

gleaming ornamental rivets, they make such a din flat-
ulating down Kings Road – the buckskin fringes of their
saddlebags flapping in a dirty breeze – that nobody's
remotely likely to turn right without knowing they're
there. I have to stop myself from shouting out, 'Get
yourself a Porsche, you big wally!' I have an urge to run
after them down the road, though if I do I know I'll be
weeping as I bellow, 'Stop pretending to live on the
edge, you poser. *Safety freak!*'

I used to get very depressed about my prospects. The
only times I felt really hopeful were days when there
had been light showers after a long dry spell, you know,
those days when even the air seems to feel refreshed.
On that sort of day the world seemed to be full of lurking rainbows. There were rainbows everywhere, just
beneath the surface. Showers after drought: those are
the most treacherous conditions for bikers, according to
the handbook. The moisture draws built-up deposits of
oil up to the road surface, in smeary rainbows.

Even if bikers were passing on their kidneys left right
and centre, that didn't mean anyone else was entitled to
receive them. That was the maddening part. The crucial
factor was the proportion of people carrying donor
cards, which must be lower among bikers than in any
other section of the population. Why would anyone
climb on to a murder-cycle, which is first and foremost a
self-murder-cycle, unless they thought they were
immortal?

What I was looking for was a personality profile as
unrealistic as anything you'd see in a small ad. *Polycystic*

kidney owner, half insane with renal thirst, renal desire, seeks risk-addict with a social conscience for anonymous but committed relationship. Devil-may-care altruist biker ideal. Long-fitting leather jacket with padded panel preferred. What I needed was someone with no thought for the future, who had contemplated the relocation of his organs after death.

To express my prospects visually, use a Venn diagram. Draw a circle. Write inside it the number of biker kidneys surrendered by their owners over a given period. Draw another circle. Write inside it the number of people in the country who carry organ donor cards. Now the only question is: do your two circles overlap, and if so by how much? Is it a substantial swathe, or the merest shared rind? Do your circles seem to push each other apart, the way mine would always do, as if they carried opposite magnetic charges? As if we would never be allowed to meet, me and my destined kidney.

You'd think there would be solidarity among kidney disease sufferers, but I can't say I ever noticed any. Rather the reverse. Mind you, the only people I met with similar conditions to my own were the people before and after me on the dialysis machine. It's not a social occasion, of course, but the routine is pretty constant and you get to know the faces. The person who followed me on the machine, I have to admit, I barely remember. It was in the nature of things that I should be raring to get out of there and get on with my life, in the few hours that it seemed that I actually had one. I took my temporary energy away from the renal unit just as fast as I could, and I set about doing whatever it was that I wanted to do while I was still able to do it. The last thing I would want to be wasting mental energy on, when I was at my brief peak, was a sick person with the sallow look of renal need, dragging his carcass towards the machine.

With my predecessor on the machine, the positions were reversed. He would sweep past me on the way to his life, hardly sparing a glance for a fellow sufferer, but I got to know him well enough. His name was Charles Earwin, which stuck in my mind because it was only one letter away from Charles Darwin. Summer or winter, he always wore a double-breasted suit. What sort of man wears a double-breasted suit for an appointment with a machine?

It was strange. Even across the energy gap that existed between us, which would have masked much, there was a definite crackle of antipathy. I remember feeling elated when I thought, one week, that he was looking a little yellow. I thought he might be going down with hepatitis, and it cheered me right up, even though I already knew that his blood group, like Terry's, was O. We weren't in direct competition for donors, and yet I was glad of anything that would tend to disqualify him from receiving a transplant. In some renal units and some health authorities, hepatitis is enough to disqualify you all by itself. Even if he wasn't disqualified, he'd be put on a separate machine, in isolation, and I'd have had someone else on the machine before me, someone else to make me bristle. But if Earwin was disqualified, I would be glad.

It was an astonishingly primitive emotion. At some level way below logic, Earwin and I were a pair of mangy lions, ancient rivals, staking out the same clearing, waiting for some teenaged wildebeest to fall off his Honda.

I was trying to explain this primitive emotion to Terry, or I think I was, in the garden one Sunday afternoon, when I was struck by lightning. I'll never know for sure what I was going to say, I have to guess from what Terry remembers me saying immediately before I was struck down. I like the idea that the discharge short-circuited not only my short-term memory, but also the flight recorder. Perhaps at the moment the lightning struck even the black box turned white with the flash, and whatever was in my head at that moment went unrecorded.

Our house, our last house, had a funny little garden that we'd made from scratch. The house was one of those up-down houses, built on a hill, where the back door is on the first floor, if you see what I mean, relative to the front. The land sloped so steeply that you'd have to call the garden a cultivated precipice, really, rather than a garden proper, but somehow we'd managed to install a fish pond. We kept some koi and some golden orfe, which you're not supposed to do in the same body of water, but we went ahead anyhow. The thing is that they're susceptible to different diseases and need to be given different medicines, and then for instance the orfe can't tolerate the treatment you have to give the koi for sores, and so on.

We solved that problem by putting the orfe in a big plastic dustbin – with an air-pump, naturally – while the koi were getting their medicine. Then the only problem was that one of the neighbourhood cats somehow smelled the orfe in their isolation tank, and would balance with three paws on the edge of the dustbin, using the other paw to scoop fillets out of the orfe as they milled helplessly about in their barrel. We lost quite a few of the orfe before we worked out what was happening. It's a wonder the cat didn't fall in, didn't lose its footing and drown in the sushi pool.

Anyway, after the koi had finished their course of treatment, and the orfe were back in the little pond with them, I thought they were owed a bit of a spring clean. Sunday was not my best day for even the lightest chores, but I gave it a go. On Sundays the itching of my skin was at its worst. It seems to be a symptom that puzzles people with functioning kidneys. They can get their minds round the idea of kidney failure and dialysis dependence, and they can even grasp in a theoretical way the price that you pay for being on the machine. But if you mention the itching, as far as they're concerned it just doesn't add up. Why should kidney failure make you itch? It's as if they're waiting for me to say, Of course you're right, that must be something different. I must be allergic to church bells or *Desert Island Discs* or the Sunday papers. Instead I explain, as patiently as I can, that I'm not an expert, I'm only a sufferer, but I do know that I begin to itch the day after dialysis, and on a Sunday afternoon I'm a twitch with a chance resemblance to a human being.

On a Sunday I wouldn't be feeling like doing anything, but at least if I was doing some chore or other I'd have something in my hands to distract me, and I wouldn't have to work so hard fighting the urge to scratch. On Sundays even doing the dusting felt like operating heavy machinery, so I suppose it shows I was really rejoicing along with the cured koi – and the orfe returned from exile and feline marauding – that I tried my hand at some work in the garden.

The weed had got out of hand. The pond was fairly choked with it. As I got down to work, Terry was sitting cross-legged by the pond with a bowl on his knees, shelling peas. From what he told me afterwards, I may have been on the point of telling him about the primitive emotion that I felt for Earwin. That I should be struck by lightning at just that moment makes it seem almost as if I was breaking a cosmic rule and must be silenced, my memory wiped.

The lightning was self-inflicted, of course. I had cut into the power line leading from the house to the garden shed with my secateurs. The circuit-breaker did its job in a fraction of a second, but for that fraction we received quite a lot of electricity, the fish and I.

Terry was looking away at the moment that I cut into the power line. When he looked up, I was on my knees several feet uphill from the pond. I still don't know how I got there.

Terry was by my side in seconds. He grabbed hold of my hands, and he was saying, 'Do you have any idea how much I love you, One-take? Do you have any idea?'

Apparently, how your body reacts to an electric shock has a lot to do with what phase of its action your heart happens to be in at the time. Systole and diastole, those are the technical terms, aren't they? Well, whichever one is the lucky one, though actually I think the lucky state is a half-way house perfectly poised between the two, that's what my lucky heart happened to be doing. In fact I felt rather good for a little while. The electric shock I had received turned out to be the next best thing to a home dialysis kit. I felt the way I imagine people feel after taking vigorous exercise – people who are well enough to take it.

I couldn't take my eyes off the peas that had fallen from Terry's bowl when he ran to be by my side. The bowl, of white enamel, had falled upside-down. The shelled peas, meanwhile, had rolled some way down-hill, while the emptied pods lay close to where they had fallen. The pods yet to be shelled showed an intermedi-ate pattern of behaviour, rolling over only once or twice before lying still. In their random-seeming but deeply ordered distribution against the grass they made a daz-zling display of different grades of green – the paleness of the pods, the rich but subtly mottled tone of the peas themselves, which showed fleeting highlights of yellow. The dull colour of the grass seemed by contrast like the studiously subdued velvet lining of a jewel case.

I just gawped at the scattered vegetables. We had all obeyed physical law in our different ways, the laws governing peas that roll from a bowl, the separate subsections concerning pods full and empty (with the exemption from rolling), the laws that apply to men who stand in ponds to sever power lines with secateurs.

Terry meanwhile was subject to the laws that govern lovers who see their loved ones lightning-struck. My lover knelt below me on a grass slope spangled with peas and their pods. He held my shaking hands in hands that also shook, and he asked again: 'Do you have any idea how much I love you, One-take?'

I for my part was inspired by electrocution, and I came up with a response that met declaration with declaration but also reached into the past to clear up something that had hung there unresolved for far too long. I said, 'Of course I do; I love you too; please don't call me by that nickname ever again; I hate it.'

My lightning euphoria lasted only for an hour or two. It was only a brief episode of synthetic health. For normal people I gather it can go on for a couple of days. But then my kidneys always knew how to drag my heart's elation down.

Oddly enough, it was the fish that showed the most lasting effects from the experience we shared. After a few weeks we noticed that several of them were swimming on one side, seeming unbalanced or confused. The symptoms weren't confined to either the orfe or the koi, and after a few days we were worried enough to make enquiries at the local pet shop. And they weren't much help at first, but then they looked the symptoms up in a book and they asked, had there been a thunderstorm around our area just lately? It was only then that the penny dropped. I'd subtly traumatized our fish when I cut the wire. They had a neurological hangover from the lightning I'd called up from the ground.

I thought I'd get through life without knowing anything about the nervous systems of fish. Funny the odds and ends you pick up on your way, titbits of science to stick next to the recipes in your scrap-book.

That was the death I wanted for myself, struck down in the pond while my ornamental fish trailed their veils and my lover shelled peas. But of course I only say that because I survived it, and had the benefit of that long moment of obituary clarity, with everything laid out and understood, Terry and the grass and the upturned bowl of peas. The only thing that died when lightning struck the pond was a name I hated and had long wanted to abolish. It was fitting that it should go at that moment, quite apart from the fact of my hating it. Death was not, as it turned out, something I could do in one take.

I suppose it's fair to say that Terry showed a mild, land-based version of the fish's little syndrome, even though he hadn't received a physical shock at the moment I took the ceremonial secateurs in my hand, like the lady mayoress at a garden fête. He hadn't even been watching when I cut the electric ribbon hung with dark green weed and declared eternity open, if only in rehearsal, but he too lost his balance for a few weeks.

He became rather clingy, and wanted me to sleep in his bed, which really wasn't practical. So I bought him the dog, a beautiful black Labrador bitch, to keep him company.

Lacquer slept in Terry's room right from the start, though it was me that took her for walks most of the time, and I was responsible for the little bit of training that she had. I was brought up with dogs and was comfortable around them, but for Terry, Lacquer was a novelty, and something of a passion.

I used to take Lacquer to the nearest patch of park, and inevitably found myself embroiled in acquaintance-ships with other dog owners – the worst sort of acquaintanceship since you can't hope to deny what it is you have in common. You can't really pretend to be taken up exclusively with your dog, to the extent of not noticing anything else, the way you could even with a toddler. Besides, the animals' bottom-sniffing sets up an expectation of some roughly similar social manoeuvre between their owners.

There was one terrible woman in late middle age, I remember, very steely and genteel, who came to the park with her benighted dog. Some people can put you off moss green for life. She introduced herself to me and to Lacquer by saying, with great imperiousness and no hint of humour, 'Kindly inform your dog that I am not in point of fact a rabbit.' It was true that Lacquer could be obstreperous in those early days, and I duly quiet-ened her down. It was only after a little while that I realized that there are some people who should in the nature of things be barked at, and if I had curbed this natural response in Lacquer then perhaps I should take it up myself.

The witch in the park disciplined her dog, a depressive mongrel called Roy, with a bottle of washing-up liquid refilled with vinegar. Roy looked to me like a genetic dead-end, a walking, drooling reproach to his parents' desire – whoever they were. If you narrowed your eyes, you could just about see that his chassis was dachshund, more or less, with terrier coachwork.

I dare say the vinegar in the witch's bottle was much diluted, but that's no excuse. I have to admit I never actually saw her use this ultimate weapon, but then she didn't need to. The way Roy flinched when she gestured with the plastic bottle made it very clear that he knew from experience what was inside it. Somehow I got the impression that poor Roy was named for a man – ex-husband the most likely candidate – who had slipped the witch's leash and put himself beyond the range of her vinegar.

Lacquer hardly needed even the conventional disciplining. She had all the biddability of her breed, and she gave Terry all the companionship he could have wanted.

He was unfamiliar with dogs and their pure blackmailing monogamy. It never stopped giving him pleasure that when he came into a room she would greet him, getting off my lap on the sofa if that was where she had been installed, as if she was choosing him each time afresh from an unlimited range of options.

I was used to the way the smell of a dog's fidelity permeates a house, spreading outwards from its basket and its blanket and its well-chewed toys, until you are never outside that faithful aroma. Dogs are condemned to finding their lives meaningful so long as you look on them with favour. Their ears must twitch every time you stir in your seat. Day after day you meet the same devoted eyes, eyes that are unable to tire of you, until one day you see that they are blind and full of pain, and you understand that you are about to make a phone call and arrange a death. Then for a while there is only the doggy smell clinging even to curtains and furniture far from the dog's actual reach, the reproachful whiff of a life that has been used to give a home its flavour.

But for Terry it was all new, it was chocolate drops and collars, shiny new discs crisply engraved with Lacquer's name and our address. When I gave Lacquer to Terry I gave him a hobby, a companion and a consolation. Giving her to him also gave me more time to myself, which perhaps I wanted, without being conscious of it. It wasn't that I bought off Terry's attentiveness when I gave him the dog, but I certainly made use of the time that I bought for myself.

When I had read the police motor-cycling method a few times, I laid it aside and went back, of course, to the Peter Hunter archive. The deeper, longer obsession forgave and swallowed up the shallow one of recent date. My biker-watching phase was just a rock-pool of fixation, and the tide came in and covered it over. My loyalty to the Peter Hunter archive was so absolute that in a strange way I didn't need to demonstrate it. I could leave envelopes with the Edinburgh postmark unopened for days or even weeks, until I had the leisure to process them properly. I needed time to absorb the subtle storm of confirmations and contradictions which the new envelopes would inevitably contain in them.

The early period almost doesn't count. Certain themes are sounded that will become important later on, but that's the most you can say. Peter Hunter wasn't calling the shots until he set up his own company. He was learning his craft, as everyone must.

It's not even that the acts change, over the years, but the meaning of the acts certainly does. In the period that was coming to an end when Peter Hunter was getting his start, but with which he overlapped in his early days, the men having sex with each other have fixed smiles throughout, the sort you learn in jazz-ballet classes. They ejaculate grinning. It's all good-hearted. For these men and the men who bought the magazines to look at them, the idea that what they're doing is vicious has been shed so recently that a ghost of it is still present in their minds somewhere. They still feel the need to counteract it, so nothing is allowed to be dirty. Every position, however extreme, is presented as if it was part of a conversation, essentially a communicative act. Yes, he's got his tongue up my arse just at the minute, but we're both still smiling the smile. It's all good-hearted. All pals.

Nastiness comes later, for almost half a decade, aggression and fearless wallowing. Then strangely enough Peter Hunter went off on a curious tack of his own. Magazines with The Pure Net copyright started to specialize in a bizarre device called the vacuum pump. It wasn't even a sex toy, more like a hi-tech version of the sort of penile enlarger that used to be advertised in the back pages of men's magazines under the headline MEN − IT CAN BE DONE. So Peter Hunter and his colleagues would stand around in groups wired up to these vacuum pumps, which looked for all the world like huge glass condoms. Occasionally someone would go down on his knees for a closer look at the depressurized tissue, perhaps even to run a ceremonial tongue along the glass.

None of them needed the help a vacuum pump was supposed to give, and I have to say the whole thing seemed to me about as thrilling as a Tupperware party. But I had been loyal to Peter Hunter for too long to give up on him in a hurry. He deserved better than that. I managed to suppress my mental protest, confronted with these men and their pumps, of *Cocks not big enough, boys? Try telling that to Terry*.

Actual condoms, as opposed to these oversized glass models, made only intermittent appearances in the magazines. In the world of Peter Hunter, they had no real place. People have dreamed about all sorts of strange things, since dreaming started, but it's safe to say that no one has ever dreamed about wearing a crash helmet, a seat belt or a condom. In the magazines, condoms made sense only as an extra perversion, never as a good resolution. The actors seemed to have no confidence in using them, none of the panache they showed with a whip or a pair of handcuffs, or with one of their ludicrous vacuum pumps, come to that.

In due course the Tupperware craze passed. I dare say I wasn't the only disappointed member of the fan club, and the sales manager of THE PURE NET® enterprises gave the creative director a good talking-to. Never mind that they were the same person, at least in my head. Peter Hunter's photo sessions became fully carnal again. Porn actors had traditionally ejaculated outside the orifices that had preoccupied them until moments before, but I suppose that was a rather poor approximation to safe sex. And of course what they did while the cameras were rolling was no guide to how they behaved in real life.

This time, when the carnality came back, so did the smiles from an earlier era, but with a difference. Now the smiles occurred not during sex but afterwards, and they were smiles of tragic solidarity. In a section at the back of some magazines, the actors who had been seen in a ferocious encounter, stags in springtime locking horns in a frenzy of rut, would be shown grinning and hugging, with the come still wet on their backs and their bellies. They all but shook hands to show there were no hard feelings. Backstage they were brothers.

Then one day I opened one of the packets from Edinburgh and read some sentences that I couldn't get out of my mind. The magazine wasn't actually a Peter Hunter production but it had an interview with him, and photographs properly credited to The Pure Net. It wasn't in fact the first time I'd seen an interview with Peter Hunter, but in the past I'd managed not to read them. I would just look at the photographs to see if there were any that I didn't have in the archive. But this time I was thrown by the headline: *A Heart Bigger Than A Hard-On*. That's a striking phrase, if not actually an elegant one, and it took me by surprise.

In my state of mild disarray I couldn't help taking in a phrase or two here and there in the article. From what I read, it seemed that Peter Hunter was doing live shows in the States, and that he was careful in the course of these entertainments to emphasize the importance of safe sex. From the stage he delivered something that was described as a hot safe sex rap. Peter Hunter referred in the interview to his educational ambitions, to his pride in being a role model, and to his sense of responsibility to the community that he served. That was what my mind took on board before I was able to hurry it back to its proper concerns.

That magazine sowed a seed of fear that took its time to sprout. Just bringing Peter Hunter and safety too close together made it possible to think the unthinkable: Peter Hunter at risk. Nothing was stopping me from going back to the interview and reading every word of it. That would have been the sensible thing to do, if what I wanted was hard information about Peter Hunter's health. But to me, Peter Hunter wasn't words. Peter Hunter was pictures. I threw that magazine away without looking at it again, the only time I can ever remember rejecting any part of what Peter Hunter offered.

There was nothing to worry me for over a year. Then it occurred to me that Peter Hunter was beginning to wear more clothes in his sessions. He'd appeared in a wide variety of costumes over the years, of course, but now it seemed to me almost that the costumes were taking over. In the past, the convention was that Peter Hunter and his co-stars might start off a scene quite elaborately dressed, but they would be stripped down to the buff – or as close to it as his fastidious sense of continuity and narrative logic would allow – when it came to coming time. Now the costumes seemed to be more persistent. Oh, of course, buttons would be unbuttoned, zips unzipped, and Peter Hunter's sexual skittle would come reliably into play. But it seemed to me that I hadn't seen Peter Hunter's buttocks, for instance, no trivial aspect of his stardom, for many months.

Looking back over the year's work in detail, I found two occasions where Peter Hunter's trousers were pulled down – the trousers of a three-piece suit in April, leather jeans in September. On past form the camera was due to pay extensive homage to his buttocks. Yet on both occasions they were obscured by another pair, buttocks of infinitely less intrinsic interest. Buttocks without a history. Buttocks that belonged in the background of the image.

One such occasion might count as a striking variation

of formula. Peter Hunter's past work was full of such coups. To be fair, it wasn't hard to imagine the urgency of lust in the mind of his co-star, pressing desire not to be satisfied by looks alone. If Peter Hunter's backside didn't magnetize your eyes, you would hardly have bought the magazine. Peter Hunter's sexual partner in the April issue, the man with the timely buttocks, had been convincingly directed to look eager. He was caught on the point of a fierce impatience; he was in a famish of lust. Why wouldn't he be following the dowsing rod of his erection towards a hidden spring, thirsty water buried in the body? It was all very eloquently done, no question about that. Work had been done and care taken. But two sequences storyboarded in the same way told a different story.

And then after all that, after all my worry, Peter Hunter's buttocks came out of their eclipse only two months later. Relief made me almost hysterical. A pimple! That's all it was! Nothing more sinister than that. But then there came a darker thought, and a relapse into anxiety. Two buttock-pimples inside a year? That wasn't like Peter Hunter's great days. That didn't sound like the radiance of which I was connoisseur. Still, I could relax a little. I could take my paranoia down a notch or two.

But although my first worries were unfounded, I wasn't wrong to worry. I still had the impression that the trend was away from full nakedness. My fear nagged and nibbled at me, and I could do nothing about it. Then I realized I could in fact do a rudimentary sort of statistical analysis, without undertaking any more research than I had already done without even thinking about it. All I had was some boxes of index cards cataloguing the archive by co-star, by sexual act and by costume, but that might be enough.

I set to work, dating and cross-referencing. Strangely, though, no trend emerged from my analysis. I puzzled over this. One explanation might be that the difference lay not in what Peter Hunter started out wearing, but how much he kept on till the end of a scene. That was a nuance of evasion that my primitive methodology couldn't hope to nail.

Then I realized something else. When I first started breaking down my data and filling out index cards, I had had to come up with a working definition of costume. Was Peter Hunter 'in costume' as a fireman if he was wearing a pair of rubber hipboots and the appropriate helmet, and waving a fireman's axe around? It seemed to me undeniable that although he would be liable to arrest for indecent exposure if he went out on to the street like that, in terms of the genre in which he was working he was indeed in costume. But clearly there was a line to be drawn, or my index cards would never be properly satisfactorily filled out. Take away the axe, and is he still in costume? Then take away the helmet. Clearly at some point it becomes nonsensical to talk about such a thing as costume.

Peter Hunter wearing the helmet and nothing else was no more 'in costume' as a fireman than I was in drag when I put on a pair of my Mum's old glasses, on evenings that Terry was working and I was depressed or out of sorts. I didn't need any vision-correction – my eyesight was fine – so I wore them low on my nose, the earpieces not firmly hooked on but resting lightly on the tops of my ears. Yes, it was silly, but I found it comforting to catch sight of my Mum's old glasses if I happened to be passing a mirror, on the nose that is just like hers, a feature that my father had no hand in.

When Peter Hunter was wearing less than a certain quota of items, it made no sense any longer to classify him as being in costume. The logical category beyond that point has to be Naked With Accessories. But I had to define that certain quota. So I established the minimum standard of costume, just for my own purposes, as three consistent items of dress, no matter what they covered or left uncovered. Pairs of gloves or shoes counted as two items, though I found it more sensible to include spurs as parts of the boots to which they were attached. If Peter Hunter had ever worn spurs on bare feet, he would have given me a headache, and I would have had to rethink my methodology. But I had what was at least a working model for a definition.

So if Peter Hunter was wearing so much as a pair of buckskin gloves and a Stetson, then in the eyes of the archive at least he was dressed as a cowboy.

In fact it was only in his immature work, before he was able to choose his own direction, that Peter Hunter went in for anything so kinky-silly. Year by year, as he took more control, he insisted on higher standards of authenticity in matters of setting. If a scene was set in the Wild West, the setting would look remarkably like a working ranch. There would be no sign of the usual tatty botching, perfunctory location shots and then a brisk cut to what looked like a motel bedroom, with a moose head propped up where the television had been until a moment before, the branching horns hinting at the aerial whose place they had so recently taken.

Part and parcel of the drive towards authenticity was an attention to detail in matters of dress. My analysis would have to separate out two unrelated curves of change superimposed on the same stretch of graph. There had been a movement towards fuller costume even before the suddenly accelerated trend that had caught my notice.

In Peter Hunter's perfectionism in matters of dress, I had come to think I could detect two factors contributing to the single complex shape of his determination never to sink to amateurishness. I felt I could detect pride and a buried memory of shame, pride denying shame, shame giving pride its edge. When Peter Hunter was just starting out in the business, standing there as a mechanic in overalls so bright and uncreased his mother might have ironed them that morning, and with a single oil-mark artistically placed on his cheek, that streak of butch blusher must have burned him like a brand. No wonder he vowed to raise the standards of the industry in which he spent his life.

One of the things I had noticed about Peter Hunter's work, even early on, was that it contained no fantasy sequences. Oh, it was all fantasy, I see that, but it was always matter-of-fact fantasy. I'm talking about something a little different. Not once in his whole career – and I'm in a position to be very definite about this – not once did Peter Hunter take part in a scenario where a teenager fell asleep over a sports magazine and then found himself bathed in a pearly light, licking jockstraps in a locker room. Peter Hunter must have been offered any number of such assignments in the early days, and the money would have been tempting, but for him I imagine it was a point of principle. The underlying assumption of all his work is that what you want can really happen – which is more likely, I dare say, if you happen to look like Peter Hunter.

As the production values of the magazines increased, the photography also changed, not in standard but in character. First it became super slick, and then it acquired a subtle roughness, like the black-and-white they sometimes use in colour magazines for grim subjects. I found this style off-putting at first, the equivalent in photographic technique of designer stubble, but later I warmed to it, with its arousing suggestion that sex is at least as much a scuffle as a ballet. All right, a choreographed scuffle, if you insist. There must always be choreography.

But now, reviewing the evidence, I began to fear that a stylistic evolution that I had come to admire might be masking physical changes in Peter Hunter that I could hardly bear to think about. The thing had to be faced. The graininess of the images, the increasingly full wardrobe – what if they were there, if not to start with then at least now, simply to distract attention?

Once it had occurred to me, this was a corrosive suggestion. A scene where Peter Hunter wore full leather, for instance, and was cruel, would once upon a time have seemed like a treat, since there is a theoretical pervert in my head who thinks himself capable of enjoying anything. But now leather wasn't a symbol of authority, it was something horribly literal. It was only a certain square footage of dyed skin that might be allowing Peter Hunter to conceal . . . what?

I was concerned enough to devise a different method of processing the information I had in the archive. I did two sketches of a human form, labelled them FRONT and BACK, and plotted on these stand-ins the areas of Peter Hunter's body displayed by one particular magazine, an old favourite. Its date was 1983, and coverage – by which I mean revelation – turned out to be total. This method of tabulating information seemed to be effective, and involved no great effort. Over the next few months, I made similar charts for every magazine in the archive.

Now I had hard evidence, which is why I put off for so long the moment of collating it. I already had a pretty clear idea of what I would find. This wasn't like the buttock-pimple panic of 1987. This wasn't a false alarm. There were serious things at stake. In a magazine dated August 1988, Peter Hunter showed the soles of his feet to the world for the last time.

I pored over those few square inches of skin with a

magnifying glass on their last appearance, before that part of the world went dark. They were flexed in pleasure, the little toes clear of the floor. To the left of the left foot, and to the right of the right, was the ridged and cleated sole of an army boot, brutish surfaces that emphasized the already extraordinary expressiveness of Peter Hunter's feet. Even with the help of my magnifying glass I could detect no irregularities in the soles of those feet. Or rather, I could detect nothing but irregularities. I looked so hard and so long that I lost all sense of what was being represented. Peter Hunter's feet became abstractions; they sank into meaningless dots. Is it true that people who drown sink feet first, following their feet down into the depths? I felt that Peter Hunter's image was drowning before my eyes.

Yet my magnifying glass could see nothing. The only evidence that there was anything at all to find was the fact that Peter Hunter made this part of his body abruptly private. In March of 1989 the same thing happened with a patch of his left thigh. His *thigh*. His lovely thigh. I could spot no blemish on its firmness, in the frozen moment before it disappeared, but I had always known that Peter Hunter was some sort of perfectionist. He would not willingly be part of anything second-rate. He was retiring piecemeal as he came to fall short of his own standards of excellence, but he still went on doing what he did. He can't have been short of money, by this stage. He just went on doing what he wanted to do, even what he needed to do.

At some time in 1989, there started to be a new feature

in Peter Hunter magazines, a portfolio of relatively orthodox pin-up poses in a section at the back. These nicely balanced the trend towards graininess in the rest of the issue, and seemed to contradict my fears. Here was Peter Hunter in a more relaxed mood. If he wore clothes, it wasn't costume but what he 'really' wore, in real life. Here he was, hanging out in a pair of shorts, or posing in a swimming-costume by the pool – the pool, presumably, that The Pure Net enterprises had enabled him to buy and fill and chlorinate and filter. On these pages he was glamorous rather than carnal. It was astonishing that he was able to project such an air of casual untouchability, when in the rest of the magazine he was always either transgressing other people's boundaries or being comprehensively violated himself.

The pin-ups were good of their kind, even exceptional, but by now I could take nothing in Peter Hunter's world at face value. After a while it seemed to me that they were the exact equivalents, in glossy photography, of medical certificates. The camera gave Peter Hunter a clean bill of health. And why not? Because it was a lie. If I had included those sections of pin-up in my chart-making, I would have been deceived into thinking that all was well. On these pages, apparently, Peter Hunter's body was once again in the public domain, without restrictions. But now that I knew what I had learned from my charts, I knew better.

At some moment of good-enough health, and with the help, quite possibly, of a make-up artist, who knows, perhaps an army of stylists, it was clear that

Peter Hunter had set up the photo session to end all photo sessions. He must have let his hair grow for a few weeks, and then had it inflected a hundred ways, with little trims that took him little by little, between rolls of film, all the way back to a crew cut. He had never dabbled much in facial hair, but he must have grown a little beard for this special purpose, and then he had that too shaped, taken down through all the gradations of stubble. And in between snips of the scissors and passes with the beard trimmer, he must have been working through his entire wardrobe. What he was trying to do was build up an inexhaustible stockpile of images of himself in peak condition, and in every possible combination of setting and dress style. It was his insurance policy, to enable him to go on working as long as possible. His longevity in the business was already extraordinary, and he was doing everything in his power to extend it.

Once I had seen through the trick, it was hard to imagine that I had ever been fooled, and that there were any number of people out there still being fooled. It made me almost angry, the cheek of it. When Peter Hunter's hair was longer, he had the facial hair. There were no pictures of him with the longer hair, and clean-shaven. And there were no pictures of him with short hair and anything longer than stubble on his face – for the simple reason that the two sorts of growth were being shortened turn and turn about. I could assemble the marathon photo session in strict sequence, though the photographs were scattered at meticulous random through a run of magazine issues. I felt I could even fix the point when Peter Hunter got tired and took a break, from a certain recurring flatness in the eyes.

There was one image that I found particularly haunting. Peter Hunter was holding up a T-shirt bearing the slogan *Age and cunning will always defeat youth and strength*. He was wryly smiling, but it seemed to me that there was something intensely melancholy about the photograph. He was holding the T-shirt, not against his body as you would if you were looking in a mirror and trying to decide whether it suited you, but over to one side, as if his public would assume his chest was worm-eaten unless it was on constant show. There seemed to be a premature capitulation in the choice of slogan by a man who can't have been more than thirty-six. Yes, he had been at the top a long time, but no one looking at him would have thought he was in anything less than his prime.

Which of course was the whole reason for those photographs to exist, to give that impression of confidence in the future, so it seemed all the more perverse to include a T-shirt that undermined it, however charmingly. I was trying to think straight, but my emotions were confused. Part of me wanted to believe that Peter Hunter was in the pink, wanted nothing better. I hadn't needed my magnifying glass to see through the ruse of the marathon photo session, but now I felt that I owed it to Peter Hunter to get it out of its case, and to conduct a search for any contradictory evidence that I might have missed when I was meeting naked flesh with naked eye.

What I was looking for was some clue that had been prepared for me alone, like the precisely adjusted wristwatch that had given me so much innocent excitement, those years ago. I was looking for a detail that would fix a date later than mid-1988. I was looking for the equivalent of the newspaper masthead that hostages hold beneath their haunted faces to prove that they are still alive, in the photographs their captors send to the press or the police. The clues that I was looking for, though I knew they didn't exist, would have carried a different message: that Peter Hunter wasn't being held hostage after all, by a terrorist that his bloodstream could only carry round and round his system, and would never be able to purify away, however sturdily his heart pumped, however devotedly his insides went about their business.

After I'd put the magnifying glass back in its case, I found myself continuing to look at the photograph of Peter Hunter holding the T-shirt. Its slogan was so defiant and humorous and also, somehow, so completely beaten. Age and cunning will always defeat youth and strength. I even tried rearranging the letters, using tiles from a Scrabble set, as if this might be another anagram, one more message in a private register. But the trouble with having so many words to work with, on an anagram, is that after a while the whole thing turns into a sort of Rorschach blot. You start finding what you want to find, until you're brought up short by the vowels running out. It seemed to me that my fingers were sorting the tiles with magic spontaneity, without my help, until I saw with a constriction of the chest that I had spelled out *Your healing heat can't fade unless I* . . .

Unless I what? It seemed less like a message from Peter Hunter to me than one sent in the opposite direction, and in any case it left a whole slag-heap of consonants unaccounted for.

After that I could only do what I had been putting off for so long, and wonder what Peter Hunter was really thinking when he held out that T-shirt and put work into his smile. In a way, that moment of wondering should have marked the end of the pornographic emotion, except that the imagination is always more flexible than people give it credit for, no matter what it chooses in the end to love. What was he thinking, really?

When the familiar packages arrived from Edinburgh, and I didn't open them, I thought at first I was just waiting for some free time to devote to savouring and sorting. But when I started filing the packages away, unopened but in order, in the same pouches that I used for the main part of the archive, I had to accept that I was doing something new. I was still the curator of my private museum of Hunteriana, but I was withdrawing from it little by little as a visitor. I never let my collection gather dust, but from that point on the only way I could maintain my relationship with Peter Hunter was by not opening any more envelopes.

It wasn't that the images in the archive lost their primary potency, but they took on bitter or distracting flavours in addition. I couldn't look at early Peter Hunter without a rush of nostalgia, nor at late Peter Hunter without wondering how well he had felt the day of the shoot, whether he had had to have a little lie down between sexual assaults, the worried continuity uncle wiping his forehead with a cloth after noting down the details, so that everything would be properly seamless when the filming resumed.

Is it possible that the embargo on the archive turned my eyes outwards again into the world, and made me notice things I would otherwise have missed? One day at the renal unit I noticed a little coiled stub of printed metal on the floor, and picked it up. It was an empty tube of anchovy paste, of all things, that somebody had rolled up, the way people do with toothpaste, to force out the last pungent fraction of an inch. I asked idly who had left it there, and even before the nurse started to speak my mind had leaped to the answer. It could only have been Earwin. My first reaction was glee, the hateful reflex of glee that any misfortune of his aroused in me. First hepatitis, nearly, and now this! He must be out of the running, surely, though we were running in different heats and it shouldn't have mattered to me. I didn't see how you could eat even a smear of anchovy paste and not tax the patience of the dialysis machine. Even saying the word 'anchovy' too many times probably got you a warning.

But not so. I was quite wrong. That bastard Earwin had found a way of beating the system, not that he'd said a word about it to me. Well, I suppose we didn't really talk, but you'd think he'd drop a hint at least. It turns out that there's a place and a time where you can consume pretty much anything you want, however salty, and the machine and the medics just smile benignly at you. Not that they want you to know about it. You could pour salt straight on to your tongue from the cellar if you really wanted.

It's while you're on the machine, of course, for the first hour of your four-hour session. That's the time and the place it can't make any difference, when you're actually on the machine. Why couldn't I work that out for myself? Perhaps the doctors are supposed to tell you about this little renal loophole, only they happened to forget when it came round to my turn. Or perhaps there is a renal grapevine, and some old lag of dialysis told Earwin, and then it was his responsibility to tell me. His choice not to tell me. It was strange to think that though we hated each other he perhaps had hated me first. While I was still making up my mind.

It turned out that the bastard Earwin used to eat his anchovy paste straight from the tube. Forget about bread, toast, biscuits, he squeezed it out directly on to his tongue, actually sucking the nozzle as his fistula thrilled and the machine sourly rinsed his blood.

He'd been doing it for years. His breath must have been a torch of salts as he passed me after his dialysis. Perhaps that's part of why we spoke so little, his not wanting me to smell what he'd been up to, his smelly little secret.

Of course I couldn't wait to try out the loophole. I'd been cheated of years of little treats. I didn't lust for anchovies in particular, let alone anchovy paste. The oasis in my desert of bland sand was a bacon sandwich. A bacon sandwich was my mirage.

I brought one with me for my next appointment, naturally, a superb sandwich made with white bread, real butter and fried bacon. If there'd been any dripping in the fridge I'd have thrown that in the pan too. And still I can't really say that I enjoyed it. It was good to have something to do, even something as trivial as chewing, while the usury box of the machine was stealing the hours it took as down-payment on the hours it let me live, but I was expecting rather more than that.

A meal eaten alone isn't quite a meal, perhaps that was it. It has no substance. The event that my snack most resembled, eaten as it was in the defiant impunity of dialysis, was a midnight feast at school, and you need a whole dormitory of furtive collaborators to arrange one of those. I thought of sharing my sandwich with the nurse who attended me while I was hooked up to the machine, but that wasn't the answer. Food can only bridge little gaps, and there was a continental divide between us, her and me, as far as our attitudes to that bacon sandwich were concerned. For her, it was just one more unhealthy snack more or less. For me it was a sacrament in greaseproof paper, and I could share it only with another believer.

A renal unit isn't exactly full of *ambiance*. No tablecloths, no waiters. It'll be a while before renal units start getting their Michelin stars.

A few mouthfuls and the rite was over. Over the following weeks I tried every possible variation of ingredients, in my search for the elusive satisfaction of the bacon sandwich. Healthier bread, margarine instead of butter, bacon grilled instead of fried, bacon made by traditional processes or else from pigs that had led unusually fulfilling lives. And still in every sandwich there was an element that nullified the whole. It wasn't possible, was it, that dialysis could actually intercept the salt-particles in the bacon before they had a chance of reaching my taste-buds? What I took into my mouth in the renal unit between slices of bread might just as well have been a slice of veal, or a piece of paper for that matter. The machine desalinated every bite.

It wasn't news to me that dialysis was paradoxical. It doesn't meet the body's needs so much as neutralize them. No thirst is slaked by the machine, no fire quenched. There's no question of satisfying the hunger for health, just of eliminating it, returning it mechanically to zero.

On the bacon question, I was forced to develop a second theory. Perhaps my salt-deprived years had coincided with a broader set of changes. Perhaps there had been a general cancellation of flavour. People who ate freely from day to day wouldn't notice the encroachments, on a broad front, of a creeping insipidity. Only I, after years of abstinence, was in a position to match present stimulus with memory and detect the progressive fading of taste-sensation from the world. This was a melancholy theory.

After the failure of all my experiments, I stopped

going to the trouble of making bacon sandwiches, but I found I couldn't give up the dialysis snack as an institution altogether. I settled on a bag of crisps as the minimum binge, and here again I found confirmation of my hypothesis about the death of flavour. I remembered salt-and-vinegar crisps in particular as having an almost caustic impact on the mouth, but they too had been bleached of all tang in the years since I had tasted any. No matter what was printed on the packet, every batch seemed, by the taste, long years past its expiry date.

Dutifully munching the irregular ovals of saturated starch from their greasy packet, while the machine did its smug work, I decided that the truth was somewhere between my two earlier theories. It wasn't that the machine somehow stole the saltiness I craved, before I could get to it, nor that there was no savouriness any more anywhere, with no one noticing but me. It was more likely that my ability to taste salt had atrophied with disuse, so that saltiness was now a sensation that I could only imagine and not experience, no matter what I put in my mouth. The saline oasis was full of neutral crystals, and salt for me could only be a memory or a fantasy.

Perhaps Earwin had made the same depressing discovery himself. I didn't care. Shared experience could do nothing to reconcile a pair like us, atavistically polarized against each other. But it seemed likely. His tube of anchovy paste was only another convenient excess, like my ritual bag of crisps. He kept his secret from me, but perhaps that was its only value. Or perhaps he had already despaired of the dialytic loophole that had seemed to promise so much, when he left that squashed-up tube for me to find.

Three times a week Earwin would put on his double-breasted Prince-of-Wales check jacket after dialysis, making sure that it hung right, tweaking the handkerchief in its breast pocket so that it showed the correct peeping triangle, no more and no less. Then he would be able to walk past me self-possessed, looking as though anchovy paste wouldn't melt in his mouth.

Then one day. One day they waited for Charles Earwin to leave in his dapper costume, carried along by the life he had borrowed from the machine, and then they nobbled me. My first reaction was fear. All I could think of was that they were going to punish me, by taking me off the machine.

The thing was this. One day I had finished with my packet of no-flavour crisps, and I was playing absent-mindedly with the bag. I wasn't planning to make mischief, but there's not a lot to do when you're on dialysis, and you find yourself making your own entertainment with whatever lies to hand. So I blew up the crisp bag without really thinking about what I was doing, and when I clapped my hands round the inflated bag it was more in a mood of schoolboy nostalgia than anything else. It was also an idle little experiment, to see if I could get up enough speed for a proper impact when I could only really move one arm, the other being mortgaged to the machine.

I wasn't the nurses' favourite patient, as I may have

mentioned, but that was fine by me, they weren't my favourite nurses. Anyway, the sudden explosion of the bag made the nurse who was in theory looking after me jump and knock her head against a metal cupboard. She was pissed off and no mistake. And after that I was expecting trouble, but I hadn't really anticipated that they would punish me by taking me off dialysis for misbehaving. Talk about over-reacting.

It took me a while to grasp that they weren't thinking in terms of punishment. Taking me off the machine, yes; punishment, no. The doctor intercepted the day's bag of insipid crisps and said, with a little smile, 'I'll take those, if you don't mind. It's Nil By Mouth for you today, chum. Let's just hope it's worth it.' And what he was proposing was taking me out of the debt cycle of dialysis altogether.

They thought, they weren't sure but they *thought*, they could offer me a kidney. Fingers crossed.

Now you'd think they'd know whether they had a kidney to offer me or not. I mean, it's not the sort of thing you can lose at the back of a fridge. It's not a pot of Sainsbury's créme fraîche, after all. But they explained that the situation was rather complicated, and they were doing everything they could. They'd keep me posted. They were hoping for the best, and they had a bed ready for me once I was done with my dialysis. If there was anything I needed – toothbrush and so on – perhaps I should make a phone call and have somebody bring it in.

After I had taken this all in, and while I was having

my blood roughly scrubbed by the machine for what I was gradually realizing might be the last time, I was in a strangely heightened state of mind. I couldn't make out how much of my elevated mood was to do with the news and how much was the ordinary resented miracle of dialysis. The future slowly lost its tinge of sallowness, as I lay there thinking. Even the thrumming of my fistula began to seem like a positive thing, a sort of song.

The doctor came back when I was finishing my dialysis, but he didn't have any real news for me. The kidney was still in limbo, however that could be possible. In a way, I felt that I had no right to ask questions, being only the poor bloody patient dangling in torment, but I managed to nerve myself. This was my life, after all, as well as a stranger's death. 'Is it a biker?' I asked.

The doctor who had made me that conditional renal promise just shrugged his shoulders. 'Isn't it always?' he said.

'How old?'

He hesitated. 'I really shouldn't tell you.'

That *really* told me that he would. 'What harm could it do?'

'Nineteen.'

'Is he . . . hanging on? Is it touch and go?'

'Oh no,' he said. 'He's good and dead.' There was a sort of sigh in his voice. 'Good and dead.'

I still couldn't imagine what the problem could be, and then a horrible thought struck me. 'The kidneys aren't. . . damaged, are they?' I asked. I suddenly had visions of my donor having neglected to wear a properly padded jacket.

My donor. The phrase was magical. It gave me a glimpse of a time when I would be able to refer to him freely, with the sort of bright sorrow that says that it's all for the best. My donor. The man – no more than a boy, really – who made all this possible. This vigour that you see.

'No. It's not that. The kidneys are fine.'

'What is it, then?'

'There's a problem with them being released. The kid's parents aren't happy.'

That seemed a strange way of putting it. Parents aren't supposed to be happy when a child dies. It would take them a considerable time, I could see that – weeks, months, even years – to accept that the person they had lost was as much my donor as their son. One description was more recent than the other, one in fact was only trembling on the edge of being, but both were valid.

But that hadn't been what the doctor meant, when he referred to the boy's parents 'not being happy'. There was something odd about the accident, apparently, and the boy's parents wanted an autopsy. Meanwhile the medical staff were fighting my corner, in a way, and trying to persuade them there was nothing to be gained from a post-mortem. There was no mystery about how the boy died, in the sense that it was perfectly plain how he had acquired his injuries. It's just that no one could work out why he was doing what he was doing when the vehicle struck him. That was what they really wanted to know, and no autopsy could tell them that.

The doctor thought that the parents would come round eventually, it was just a matter of rushing them through the stages of mourning. But of course there wasn't much time. Kidneys can't wait, he told me, as if that was something I might not know.

I didn't need to have anything brought in to me at the hospital. I'd had a case packed for years. 'You never know,' I'd said to Terry more than once. 'It'll happen when we least expect it.' So I had packed a case, a sort of glorified overnight bag, and I kept it in the boot of the car. It had been sitting there for years. I'd hardly thought about it since the time I'd packed it.

It felt strange to be going down to the hospital car park to fetch the case. There was a person who was going to get in the car and drive home as usual, chained to the dialysis treadmill, but that person was no longer me. I was the person who opened the boot instead, and pulled out the case that had been waiting for this moment for so long. I was the person who was making a break for it.

In fact, it had been so long since I had thought about the case that I found that I had lost its little key. I had to force the lock. When it had given way at last and I looked inside the case, I felt as if I was opening a time-capsule and finding again the grip that I had kept packed at school, at a time when I was very unhappy and wanted to be able to run away at a moment's notice. What had been lying forgotten in the boot of the car was actually rather like a pre-adolescent's running-away case, full of equipment for a fantasy future. Still, I hadn't yet left fantasy behind, the fantasy of being miraculously rescued. My imagination of what I might need was no more reliable on the day I retrieved the case than it had been when I packed it. Nothing else occurred to me in my tense elation that I would want brought in. I couldn't see any distance into the future, but as far as I could see, I had everything I needed.

At first I thought the nurse who took me to my room was just flustered and overworked, the way they all seem to be, and then I realized that she was quite deeply upset. When she brought in the little trolley with the payphone on it, so that I could phone Terry, she bumped it rather heavily against the bed. It hadn't occurred to me that nurses could still be affected by suffering in certain circumstances. Perhaps young death is always hard to accept, young arbitrary death, unless in some way you stand to gain by it. As I did.

The nurse had a kind face. That's not as common a thing as you might expect. I almost told her so. I almost said, 'You have a kind face,' but then I thought I'd better not.

I used to be a good observer of nurses, in the days of my early dialysis, before the distinctions got blurred. I used to be able to tell the agency nurses from the regulars at a glance. Agency nurses took liberties. They risked wearing make-up, sometimes in quite elaborate schemes. They tended to leave their lips clear or only subtly accented, since even men, administrative men, senior men, will notice lipstick sooner or later. But I dare say you can do quite a lot around your eyes and men will only think you look nice, not that you've been clever with two tones of eye shadow. Sister will notice, but it's probably not worth her while to make a fuss, the way she would with her regular staff.

Then over the years everything changed, and it wasn't just the agency nurses that dared to paint their faces. I think it was a matter of morale dropping bit by bit, so that it became harder and harder for nurses to take a pride in their work. Things went so far downhill that Sister hadn't the heart to enforce the rules the way she used to, in areas that were disciplinary rather than medical. Perhaps she too felt the need, once in a while, to cheer herself up with a little bit of slap.

I'm not saying that all the distinctions got blurred. You could always tell the nurses who lived in hostels, and I expect you always will be able to, with their baked-beans-and-white-bread complexions and their suppressed giggles. It's just that nowadays you can confirm your suspicions by seeing how a nasty shade of green migrates from one pair of eyelids to another, over the weeks, and you know you can trace the infection to a shared make-up bag on the back of a communal bathroom door.

The situation I was in, the situation I suppose we were all in, could only have arisen in a hospital that had a casualty department as well as a renal unit. Normally, there's any amount of insulation that acts to prevent recipients finding anything out about donors. The organ is separated, just by the nature of the process, from the body in which it was incubated, the person it was originally serving. I think a certain amount of information is allowed to flow the other way, in the fullness of time, so that the bereaved, being told a little about the active rewarding life that their dear dead one has made possible, may be consoled and buoyed up. But in my case a lot of that insulation was missing. At that particular moment, in that particular hospital, the sound-proofing was defective. The boy's death was still reverberating through the building, and echoes of it were likely to reach me. That was always on the cards.

Looking at it another way, if the renal unit I attended hadn't happened to be part of a hospital with a casualty department, my name wouldn't have been at the top of the list for the kidney. Matches of donor and recipient are always approximate, that seems to be the nature of things, and I was coming in anyway for dialysis. They would have thought twice before sending out a call for someone with a slightly better match, when they couldn't really guarantee anything at all. I was less likely to resent being on stand-by.

All I was risking, to a certain way of thinking, was a bag of crisps. The only chip I was betting on this round of transplant roulette was a bag of crisps that gave me only symbolic pleasure anyway.

At first I took in only scraps of what the nurse told me, and what she told me was scraps in any case, being just what her friend who worked in casualty had told her in the canteen. But I did pick up one odd detail. It turned out that the biker wasn't even on the bike when he got hit.

He had parked it at the side of the carriageway, on an access ramp to the M25 of all suicidal places, and he was struck by a van as he tried to cross to the other side of the road, for no imaginable reason. There was nothing in his line of intended travel but a wizened sapling, one of a straggly line, a forlorn planting that was all the access ramp could boast in the way of landscaping. Beyond that, nothing but embankment and then motorway.

I noticed that my fingernails against my palms were a little long, and uneven. Quite suddenly I felt the need to trim them, as intensely as I've ever felt anything, and I could have kicked myself for not thinking to pack any nail-scissors in the running-away case.

There was a tap on the door, and a moment of hushed professional semaphore just out of my line of sight. Then the nurse who had been talking to me went to attend to someone else. She said she'd be back as soon as she could, whether she had any news for me or not.

When I was alone, I made a phone call home. I could have phoned Terry at work, but I didn't think it was that sort of emergency, somehow. I had the irrational feeling that the more fuss I made, the more likely I was to be disappointed. I preferred to leave a message on the answerphone explaining the situation but saying I was perfectly happy and didn't need company. It even seemed to be true, at the time that I said it, that I was happy. I told Terry that I'd had to leave Lacquer alone for much longer than I'd anticipated when I left the house, that she'd be hungry, lonely and in need of exercise. I really did think, though it sounds ridiculous to say so, that she needed him more than I did.

After I'd left the message, I was left alone with my thoughts and my situation. One particular question I could hardly avoid asking: Why did the biker cross the road? It was a riddle, I could see that, but all the same I didn't think it was a riddle I should be getting too worked up about. My priority was to stay just as relaxed as I possibly could. I had to act naturally in a wildly artificial situation, the situation of having a date with a body part that might or might not turn up, depending. I unpacked my things from the case, trying to make a soothing ritual out of the disposition of flannel, toothbrush, books. I tried to do something I'd never done before as if it was an established routine, with a routine's calming properties. Flannel, toothbrush, books. Nil By Mouth, anaesthetic, kidney.

A room with a bed in it, any room with a bed in it, is automatically more restful than a room without – even when you know that the mattress is impregnated with thickened sweat, the sweat of the sick and fearful.

I remember one Christmas when I got stuck in Selfridges during a bomb scare. The IRA were having one of their seasonal campaigns, that are really as much part of a traditional Christmas as the tree in Trafalgar Square. I was in the cologne department of Selfridges– it's funny, but there's nothing like shopping for other people to make you find presents you'd like yourself.

It's like water-divining with a credit card. You half-close your eyes, and your financial plastic tugs you along. Then you open your eyes and you think, that's not quite right for so-and-so, but it *is* rather marvellous.

I heard loudspeakers outside in Oxford Street, and at first I thought it was just policemen telling pedestrians not to cross except when the lights were in their favour, the way they do towards Christmas. Then I heard sobbing, and when I looked up I saw that two teenaged assistants from the adjoining Skin Care department were holding on to each other and weeping. Finally I saw that there were tapes outside the doors of the shop preventing us from getting out.

The suspected bomb was outside in the street somewhere. I looked around me and realized that I was in a room almost entirely filled with glass containers on glass shelves. It wasn't exactly a good place to be, at that moment. At the whim of a fuse, we might all be riddled with glass fragments of various thicknesses, not to mention sheets of ignited cologne like luxury napalm.

The shop assistants seemed paralyzed, but I moved by a sort of instinct. Selfridges isn't one of the shops I know by heart, but I passed a store guide posted up on the wall and I saw where I must go. I made my way to the bedding department upstairs, and I found a bed right in the middle of the room, as far away from any window as it was possible to be. I wish I could pretend that I had the nerve to get under the covers, but you don't stop being middle class just because you think you're about to be blown to bits. I sat down on the bed, but I found myself jiggling up and down a bit, as if I was testing the springs with a view to purchase, shopping doggedly on in the middle of a terrorist operation. Even sitting on the bed was soothing, and I was irrationally certain that I would have time to dive beneath the duvet between the moment of hearing the explosion and the arrival of the window-glass in its fragments.

Now in the room that the hospital had set aside for me while I waited, I sat down on the bed, and struggled to feel as calm as I had when I thought that flaming pieces of glass were going to start flying about at any moment.

There were a couple of packs of cards in the running-away case, and for a while I tried playing patience. I stopped when I discovered that for once I was seriously tempted to cheat, so as to make the patience come out dishonestly. That stopped me in my tracks. If I could start being superstitious about something so silly, it stood to reason that the game wasn't doing its job of distracting me from my anxiety. All it was doing was giving me a new set of symbols to feel anxious about.

I turned the radio on. It was tuned to the hospital's own station, and when the DJ came on to do his bit between records he mentioned that they were always happy to play requests. Keep those requests coming, he said, dedicate a song to someone you love. The DJ said if you wrote a request on a bit of paper and gave it to any nurse or member of staff, it would be sure to get to him.

I had been far-sighted enough to pack a notepad in

the running-away case. I tore off a sheet and wrote out a request. 'Please play "Daniel" by Elton John for Terry with love from William.' It was typical of my mind, or of things in general, that the moment I had written the name of the song on a piece of paper, its refrain came to haunt me, as if I had just heard the song and not written out a request to hear it, for the first time in months. I couldn't get the words out of my head: 'Daniel my brother, you are/ Other than me.'

It seemed such a stupid reflex to get a tune on the brain, as if I had a lower resistance to bland melody than most people. And just from writing down the name of a song! I mean, it's bad enough belching at the end of a meal, it's rude but at least it's natural. But here I was belching because I'd *ordered* a meal. It made no sense, particularly as I'd always thought Elton John's lyrics woefully bad. I'd told Terry so often enough. 'He doesn't write them,' he would always say, and I would always say, 'What kind of an excuse is that?'

I looked down at the piece of paper on which I had just written my request. Then I tore it up and wrote it out again in capitals, on the principle that anything a DJ can get wrong he will, and it's silly to take chances. PLEASE PLAY 'DANIEL' BY ELTON JOHN FOR TERRY WITH LOVE FROM WILLIAM. There still seemed to be something wrong with what I had written, somehow. Then I tore up that piece of paper too, and peeled a third one from the pad. I wrote out the message one more time, only this time with TERRY spelled TERRI instead. We can't all of us be brave all the time.

The next time a nurse came in, I passed her the piece of paper. I said under my breath, 'The condemned man's last request,' and she gave me a routine smile that showed she hadn't really heard. Condemned man or reprieved man? My status was uncertain in any case. That's what it was all about, this whole infinite afternoon.

Nil By Mouth was the least of it. That was a very ordinary deprivation. I was used to thwarting my thirst, and to thwarting my appetite for all the things that would promote thirst. And this time, with luck and a following wind, self-restraint might lead to not having to be self-restrained ever again.

Later on there was some more information about the biker, not real news, just a few more details. One of the mysterious things about the accident was that he hadn't locked the bike. He had taken off his helmet and hung it on one of the handlebars, just as if he was going to come back to it in a matter of seconds. He was still wearing the bike lock over one shoulder, like a bandolier, when he was struck. It was a heavyweight chain of oiled steel – or more exactly, I was told, some sort of arrangement of overlapping joints and flanges for protection against hacksaws – inside a thick plastic sheath. Apparently the lock contributed in some way to his injuries. The idea seemed to be that the van would have hit him like a hammer anyway, but the end of the lock was driven into him by the impact like a nail into soft wood. I don't know where it did the damage, it would have seemed, I don't know, pornographic to ask, but if it had been near the kidneys they would have said.

The driver of the van, when he gave his side of things to the police, seemed to think that the biker – his name was Gary – was moving very slowly. Just strolling across the access ramp towards a tree that had happened to catch his eye. I expect that the heavy lock and his heavy leathers, plus solid boots as so strongly recommended by the police motor-cycling method, slowed him down a fair bit. On the other hand, I think the van driver's testimony described the way time slows down in a crisis, with a little wishful thinking thrown in. What was he going to say? The lad was going like the clappers, but I managed to bag him anyway?

The fact is, the last thing you expect to see on that sort of road is a stray pedestrian. I remember my driving instructor telling me that whenever I couldn't actually see a stretch of road, I should assume that there was an old man with a handcart just out of my line of sight, and drive accordingly. But that would just have been a smart thing to say during my driving test. It hasn't ever been how people drive in real life. Old men with handcarts hiding in the hedges – why not send out a servant with a red flag in front of you, while you're at it? People always drive too fast on those access ramps, it's a fact, they've had a whiff of the motorway and it gets them all excited. I don't think Gary had much time to get out of the way.

He'd always been a good boy, according to his parents, never any trouble. He knew his parents didn't want him to get a motor bike, so between them they came to an arrangement. He brought up the subject on his seventeenth birthday, and they made him wait – hoping he'd lose interest, I expect – but they never actually said no. They'd learned from experience, or just worked out for themselves, that this was the sort of area where saying no was actually a perverse sort of incitement.

So they struck a bargain. Gary would wait till his eighteenth birthday, and he'd get holiday jobs so he was paying his whack, and he wouldn't just put his L-plates on and zoom about, he'd get proper instruction at an authorized training centre. He must promise never to ride dispatch or deliver pizza, no matter what. No matter what. Not only that, he'd go to an evening class in motor-cycle maintenance, so he'd learn that even a dream machine gets rust spots and clogged lines once in a while. Dreams need maintenance.

They also insisted that he fill out a donor card, there in the sitting-room in front of them, on his eighteenth birthday. It wasn't that they forbade him to take risks, it's just that it had to be real to him what risks he was taking. They watched as he signed the undertaking on the bright red card. I would like to help someone live after my death.

He promised his parents he would wear a proper full-face helmet. They hadn't liked him wearing a leather jacket before he got the bike, they didn't think it was really him, but after that they made him promise he'd always wear one, however hot the weather got.

Gary was never a drinker, which had given his parents one less thing to worry about. Some of his biker friends weren't so responsible, but Gary had an old head on young shoulders. Which was exactly why they were trying to block the release of the kidney I needed. They had contacted a lawyer to see what he could do to help. Their thinking went like this: Gary had done something very irrational, absolutely against the grain of a sensible character.

Not only was he no drinker, he had never smoked a cigarette in his life. And yet he had parked the motor cycle, taken his helmet off and set out on foot across a highly dangerous road, towards a sapling that was no different from its fellows except for having a cigarette packet mockingly impaled on a twig at shoulder height. It was as if Gary had been drawn irresistibly across a deadly road by an empty packet of Rothmans King Size International.

He hadn't been drunk. That was certain. He wouldn't knowingly have taken drugs of any sort. But the van driver said he was moving very slowly. What if Gary had been under the influence of a drug and hadn't even known it? What if one of his friends had slipped him something? Maybe not even maliciously, just to 'turn him on' to something new. To open his eyes.

They couldn't bring Gary back, they understood that. No one knew that better than they did. But if they could prevent what happened to Gary happening to someone else's son, that would be something. So they wanted an autopsy to confirm their suspicions, or else to put their minds at rest. Though they would never really know any peace, while Gary's death remained a mystery. They wanted an autopsy, and if the police wouldn't take action against whoever was responsible, then they would bring a private prosecution. They owed that much to Gary. What's the point of having savings, if you can't spend them on something important?

By this time I had changed into the pyjamas from my running-away case, and while the nurse was talking I had started to realize they had become musty after so long in the boot of my car. I started to wonder if the nurse couldn't in fact smell the mustiness of my pyjamas, and I felt uncomfortable enough at the possibility to move a little distance away. Of course I couldn't get very far away, in a hospital room. To cover my embarrassment, I turned on the radio. I was just in time to catch a few seconds of perky melancholy, fading out. I recognized the tune. The hospital radio station had just played 'Daniel'. My first thought was, bloody hell that was quick, they must be desperate for suggestions. But childish as it seems, I felt genuinely cheated of my request. I wanted that ratification, somehow, if you can call it that. I wanted to hear my name and Terry's read aloud, however amateurishly it was done from a technical point of view, however small or indifferent the audience.

I had been conscious that my nails needed cutting for hours by this time, and I finally got up the nerve to ask the nurse for a pair of scissors. She went and got some smartly enough, but I think perhaps she was a touch offended that I'd interrupted her with such a trivial request. She was giving me a full picture of my situation, after all, which meant she was bending the rules in my favour, and it might have looked as if I was bringing her back into line, saying Me patient, You nurse – Me need, You get. But it's funny, by that time if I'd been asked which I needed most, kidney or nail-scissors, I think I'd have gone for the scissors.

I don't remember anyone on *Desert Island Discs* ever asking for a pair of nail-scissors as their luxury on the island. I can't imagine that no one's ever thought of it. Perhaps it's like your book, where you're supposed to choose anything except the Bible and Shakespeare. Perhaps your luxury can be anything but nail-scissors, only it's so obvious that they don't actually need to spell it out.

The nurse came back with a pair of scissors, and yes, perhaps she was a little miffed. She didn't stay. When I was alone again, I kept the radio turned on, but I found I was in need of more than one distraction. I picked up one of the books that had spent so long in the running-away case. They were perfectly ordinary books, which my condition lent a forbidden quality. There was a survey of the wines of Bordeaux; a fell-walking guide; a holiday brochure. I chose the brochure.

I hadn't had a holiday since before dialysis, but I don't want to make too much of that. In a good year I was making good money, more than enough to arrange for dialysis in foreign cities, if I'd thought it was worth it. One night, sitting in front of our television, Terry and

I heard me extol in rapid succession a dog food whose contents I can't bear to think of (the one that dogs know so much about), a face cream with nonsensical ingredients – nobody at the studio could begin to tell me what liposomes were – and a building society that I wouldn't trust with a penny piece. It was a hat-trick. I'd scored a hat-trick. It was also like my bank interrupting normal programming, to let me know that my bank balance had just received three healthy kisses of credit.

But I never thought it was worth it. I didn't want a holiday with dialysis. It was dialysis I wanted the holiday from. Going abroad with polycystic kidney disease would have been like taking an imaginary dialysis machine with me wherever I went. I couldn't imagine carrying on like what's-his-name that plays the cello, strapping his instrument into the seat next to him while a zombie stewardess offers it complimentary peanuts.

Terry always hated it when I made fun of stewardesses – apparently they're all clever and deep and sweet – but that's one worry I have left behind and never need to think of again.

Lying there in my musty pyjamas with my holiday brochure, with the hospital radio station playing rock so soft it could hardly stand up by itself, I should have been comforted by the feeling that so many people, out of my sight, were working on my behalf. Admittedly, Gary's parents were standing between me and his kidney, but they had their reasons and in any case the doctors were trying to talk them round. Maybe the police were doing some investigating into the accident, though I couldn't quite imagine what it was they could be investigating at this point. An operating theatre was in readiness, and a surgeon was on stand-by, the same as I was.

And of course the kidney itself was lying in its accustomed cavity, waiting to be lifted briefly into the light and then tucked into a strange new body, where it would give and get new life.

Either that, or be burned or left to rot. Transplantation, ash or mulch. Gary's kidney stood at a crossroads, and so, I felt, did I. Every minute that passed lessened my chances of survival with Gary's kidney.

Every minute made a difference. I needed all the distraction the radio and my brochure could give me, to stop me from thinking despairing thoughts. I was afraid of finding out the hard way that transplant surgery has something in common with cooking. Everything depending on the freshness of the ingredients.

However hard I tried to persuade myself that everyone was working in my interest, in fact I felt they were all against me. The police had better things to do than reconstruct Gary's last moments alive, on the off chance that it would convince his parents to release the kidney. They had other fish to fry. They were probably all staked out in public toilets by this time, the pretty ones playing with themselves in the stalls, the homely ones waiting behind the one-way mirrors with video cameras.

On top of which, my getting Gary's kidney would only make more work for the doctors, which these days is one thing they absolutely don't need. Just one look at them will tell you that. If Gary's kidney stayed put, some overworked surgeon could get a little shut-eye, and maybe later tonight a scalpel wouldn't slip and a life would be saved. How could it be in the public interest for me to get Gary's kidney? The queue for dialysis is so long that one more or one less really doesn't make a difference. Our cries are weak, our voices choked with microtoxins. We are a choir of ghosts, huddled round the dialysis machine.

Above all, I thought the nurses, staff or agency, new arrivals and seasoned sisters, all of them, were too busy grieving for Gary – his youth, his parents' pain, the sense of waste, the heavy irony of the lock that killed him – to want anything good to come out of his death.

I don't know for a fact that Gary's parents were at the hospital at that time, but I had the strong impression that they were. It seemed to me that I could feel them somewhere near. Beyond the walls I could sense a powerful magnetic field of grief, with a male and a female core.

Then the DJ started talking between tracks in his amnesiac patter. He had the eerie knack of making something live sound as if it was pre-recorded, but for once the important thing was what he said, and not how he said it. What he said turned the world around. The Halloween hairs on the back of my neck were the first to know about it. Somehow they had advance information.

The DJ said: 'Seems like the whole Elton John Appreciation Society is in the hospital today. I don't know, maybe listening to old Elton is bad for your health (ha ha). I've got a request here from William for "Daniel", which I'm afraid we played just a couple of hours ago for Sue. Sue, I expect you're in Post-Op by now and not listening to the radio, but if you are . . . hope hearing us play your request made a difference. And William, I hope you don't mind, but I'm going to play another Elton classic, a personal favourite of mine, but then I always say that don't I. William, you don't say if Terri is your wife or your girl-friend, but you do say you send her your love. So this is going out to Terri, with love from William. With all William's love.' I heard the bite and hiss of a needle meeting vinyl, and then I heard Elton John's piano at its most eloquent, the sad-brave opening chords of 'Song for Guy'.

That was when the whole thing became real to me. That was when I realized that I was going to get Gary's kidney. I'd requested 'Daniel' and been given 'Song for Guy', which of course was what I'd really wanted in the first place, except that asking for it would have been obscene or unlucky, unlucky because obscene. But the DJ had read my mind, and had given me what I didn't dare to ask for. That day I would get what I wanted, no matter what. My prayer had been in code in the first place. I mean, 'Song for Guy' is only an Elton John track, why shouldn't I request it if I want to hear it? But it had a private meaning, and I was afraid to ask. So I substituted for it a request that was even more oblique.

And yet the prayer I'd suppressed was answered in spite of everything.

'Song for Guy' doesn't take a long time to play – that is, it's long for a single but not for an album track, maybe six minutes or so. And even before the DJ had finished playing it on the hospital radio station, the nurse with the kind face was back to tell me what had happened to Gary. There had been a secret reason for his actions after all, a hidden spring that explained everything. It wasn't a brainstorm, there was mechanism. A motor and a magnet.

The nurse was on the edge of tears, and then for a moment she was actually over the edge of tears, before she pulled herself back. I thought she was crying for Gary, but tears are never simple and it may be that she was also crying for me. For Gary's loss and my gain.

The police had done some work, despite all my fears. They had inspected the site more thoroughly and had found the keys of Gary's bike, which had been knocked out of his grasp by the impact of the van. They had missed finding the keys on an earlier search, because they had travelled so far from Gary's hand. The bike had been taken to a police depot some time before, and when the key and the bike were reunited, someone – himself a biker and a bit of an enthusiast – had the idea of starting the machine up. Nothing happened. A fuse had blown. The electrics were out.

At this point the biker policeman put his thinking cap on. In my mind as I listened there formed an image of a fresh-faced bobby taking off the regulation helmet and putting on a deerstalker cap. The hats replaced each other back and forth in my mind with an artificially out-of-focus effect, a crude dissolve.

But whatever it was he wore on his head, little by little this biker policeman worked out why Gary had crossed the road, towards a blue and white cigarette packet impaled on a twig.

It had to be Rothmans. It couldn't be Benson and Hedges. It couldn't be Dunhills, it couldn't be Camels. The list goes on and on, of brands it couldn't be. It couldn't be Marlboros, it couldn't be John Player Specials. Not Gauloises, not Silk Cut. It had to be Rothmans King Size International.

Gary needed something to patch up his electrics, to bypass the blown fuse. He must have learned how to jury-rig things at his motor-cycle maintenance evening class. That's where he must have learned the fatal detail. Only the silver paper of Rothmans cigarettes, of all the brands currently available, still has a high enough metal content, even in these straitened days, to make a workable connection. None of the other brands could have tempted him across the access ramp with their inferior conductivity. No other make will carry a charge.

A packet of chewing gum – the metallic inner wrapper of each edible stick, to be exact – might also have worked the trick and drawn him across the road to the baited tree, but how would he have been able to see it from so far off? Really, it had to be a distinctive blue and white packet, legible from a distance, stirring faintly in the breeze. Even a length of fuse wire, the very thing that Gary needed, would not have been visible, coiled round a sapling, besides looking a little providential. A little spooky.

The nurse said she was happy for me. I tried to say that I was sorry for Gary's parents, but I couldn't get the words out. Rightly or wrongly, I still felt I was being grudged the kidney by all the kind people I was dealing with. Gary's life – his youth, his A levels, his girl-friend, his bass guitar – outweighed mine in their eyes. They were going to operate on me in a little over an hour, and still they thought that I didn't have a right to benefit from Gary's death. Or that's how it seemed to me. In their eyes, Gary's kidney was a windfall – as if I hadn't been standing under the kidney tree and shaking it, for nine years athirst beyond thirst.

Nobody who hasn't been in my position can know how I felt. I didn't feel how I wanted to feel, all noble and grateful. I felt the way I felt, that's all. How did I feel? I felt like the customer in the Monty Python cheese shop sketch. That's exactly how I felt. I'm thinking of his last line but two or so, just before he says, 'In that case I'm afraid I'll have to shoot you,' and does. I may not have got the phrasing exactly right – it may have been 'kill you', not 'shoot you' – but it would be an easy thing for you to look up.

It's one of the most famous sketches in the whole of 1970s television comedy. It's been repeated endlessly on television, it's probably in one of the Python films (the first one would be the most likely guess), and it's been transcribed any number of times in Python scripts and comedy anthologies. No doubt about it, the BBC has done very well out of that particular sketch.

How I felt when I knew I would be receiving Gary's kidney is perfectly expressed by the Cheese Shop Customer's line, the one before 'In that case I'm afraid I'll have to kill you' (or 'shoot you'). And if that strikes you as an ugly feeling, well you may be right, but that's out of my hands. You haven't been where I've been, or you'd understand.

I deserved that kidney. I earned it with my patience. I paid for it with my taxes, come to that. The Health Service is supposed to be free at the point of need, isn't that the phrase they bandy about at election time? If I wasn't at the point of need, what must the point of need be like? How much do you have to go through, to be given your entitlement?

Gary's death was sad, of course it was sad. Sad sad sad. It was tragic. But it wasn't as if it was my fault. Life goes on. Wasn't my own brother knocked down when he was nine, crossing the street after school to buy sweets? No, because I never had a brother, but if I had had, and he'd been killed, I would have wanted life to go on for someone else.

A man comes into a cheese shop to buy some cheese. Each time he mentions a type of cheese there's a reason why the shopkeeper can't supply it. Sometimes the shopkeeper says Yes, he has some Caerphilly, or alternatively some Mongolian yak mozzarella or some hamster Edam (I'm making that up, but there is a long inventory of absurd cheeses), but there always turns out to be a snag. There is no cheese to be had in the cheese shop, and the reasons why not become more and more grotesque. Hard cheeses, soft cheeses; blue cheeses, white cheeses; domestic, exotic. Still no luck. Finally the customer mentions Brie, and the shopkeeper says Yes, as a matter of fact he does have some Brie, in the back of the shop. The customer wants some, of course. The shopkeeper goes off to find it, but then comes back to say, no, on second thoughts the Brie is a little bit too runny to be at its best. And the customer says – it's John Cleese, it's British politeness driven to mania and despair – 'I don't care how fucking runny it is, hand it over with all speed.'

I don't care how fucking runny it is, hand it over with all speed. *That's* how I felt about Gary's kidney.

Terry arrived at the hospital a little before they put me to sleep. I'd told him not to come, and here he was on cue. I'd told him to stay at home and look after the dog, and so he'd brought her along in his shabby little car. He'd left the window open a crack, and he'd put some biscuits and a bowl of water on the floor in the back. He'd spread newspaper just about everywhere, since he didn't know how long he'd be away from her. Lacquer's toilet habits could be a bit impressionistic at the best of times, and she was sensitive enough to the human events around her to know that this was not an ordinary day or an ordinary journey.

I'd told Terry not to come, and here he was. That's the great thing about monogamy. You start off saying what you mean and meaning what you say, but nobody can keep that up for very long. Then you go through a phase for a few years where you start putting things into a code that you think is absolutely clear, and you get more and more baffled when your partner does the same thing. You end up going to a lot of parties that neither of you want to go to, if only you knew it. You've stopped communicating directly and you haven't yet learned to read each other's minds. And then finally you've worn a track through the days like a track on lino, and you're continuously aware of each other without ever needing to think about it.

Things arrange themselves, and you find that the CD collection is alphabetized, while the system with the records is that when you've played something you put it at the extreme right of the stack, and this is perfectly satisfactory but you aren't even sure there was a conversation in which it was decided that it should be so.

Until every decision is a compromise, even when you're actually trying to be selfish, you don't begin to taste the reliable elusiveness of another person in the same space, the same life, the predictability that never grows stale. I miss that. That's what I miss. I miss that.

I'd given Terry explicit instructions not to come to the hospital, and it wasn't that I was being insincere. I wouldn't have been in the least put out if he'd done as I suggested. But the moment he knocked at the door of my hospital room I knew it was him. I knew exactly the length of the interval that would pass between me saying 'Come in' and him turning the handle. I knew exactly the height that his eyes would be at, and even lying on an unfamiliar bed, my optical muscles knew exactly how to calculate the angle of incidence so that our eyes were united right away.

I'd told him in my answerphone message that I was fine for pyjamas and everything, and he'd brought a spare pair that I was glad of. They smelled fresh, they smelled of home. I'd been through so many emotions in such a short time that day that I didn't want to rehearse them all over again for his benefit, and he didn't press me. I just wanted him to be there.

Terry and I had a campy little conversation about stitches and scars. I said, 'I asked for cross-stitch but apparently that's extra.'

'Where will it be, exactly?'

'Oh, down around here, and this side, I think. Yes, I know it's one of your favourite parts, and it won't look so good next time you see it. Enjoy it while you can.'

'Lucky I've got so many favourite parts, then,' he said, and that was about it, until after the operation. Very British. If our hard-ons were anywhere near as stiff as our upper lips, we'd be world-beaters. There'd be no one to touch us.

I told him in my own way that everything was going to be all right. 'You won't mind not getting any taller, will you, babe?' I asked.

'I'll get used to it,' he said. That was our way of talking about renal osteoporosis. I'd been five eleven when I met Terry – usefully taller than his five eight – but by this time I was down to five nine. But when we talked about it we always made out that it was him that was growing, not me that was shrinking.

I never told this to Terry, but it was important to me to get my transplant and stop the rot, while I was still taller than my lover. I really clung to that height differential, for some reason – and after swearing that I don't care about size, too! I just wouldn't let it go.

Even then, before I went for surgery, I knew that Gary's kidney wouldn't work, wouldn't take, wouldn't stay. I'd been doing the sums in my head, and I knew that by the time it reached me it would be a ten-and-a-half-hour kidney. That's pushing it a bit. A kidney of that age is an iffy prospect. For eight hours after death kidneys are young and impressionable. They'll try anything. Then at eight hours old they enter a grey area, and at twelve hours old you pretty much have to bin them. So a ten-and-a-half-hour specimen like Gary's kidney was already weary of the world by the time it reached me. You can't teach an old kidney new tricks, more's the pity.

In any case, matches between donor and recipient are always approximate. What is arranged under the bright lights of the operating theatre is only ever a blind date. It's only between identical twins that there is perfect accord, no possibility of rejection, no distinction between yours and mine. It's funny, outside actual twinship there's no distinction, from a kidney-transplant-medical point of view, between a relative and a stranger.

If Gary had been my true twin, I'd have been laughing. What a stupid thing to say. I'd have been laughing through my tears. Since polycystic kidney disease is congenital, any identical twin of mine would have the identical problem. We could play musical kidneys all day long, pass the bloody renal parcel, and never be any better off than when we started.

It wasn't the actual operation I was worried about. I didn't doubt that they'd be able to install the kidney. What was it they used to say in that television series in the seventies? *We have the technology. We can rebuild him.* And you'd think that would be the end of my troubles, wouldn't you? Nice new kidney, nice new life, let the party begin.

Except that this is one party where the bouncers are downright aggressive, and they keep harassing one guest in particular. The kidney isn't on the guest list, apparently, and nothing will persuade the bouncers that it has a right to be there. The only way to keep them quiet is to spike their drinks with something called cyclosporine, which takes the edge off their aggressiveness. Even then, they go around muttering darkly, and the kidney looks worried and starts nervously fingering its invitation. And you have to judge the dosage nicely, because if the bouncers get too slap-happy they start to let just anyone in. Then nobody has any fun.

But it wasn't even that. The kidney that I was given brought A levels with it, and a bass guitar. Even a girl-friend. Oh God, the kidney had a girl-friend. Everything these days has a memory, doesn't it? You can't buy a typewriter without it having a memory. It remembers the last letter you wrote. The telephone remembers the last number you dialled. Your cash card remembers the balance of your account. And the kidney I was given, it too had its little sliver of memory. My new organ was full of old echoes, of resentments and regrets.

I didn't choose this young man's kidney. Do you think, if I could choose, that I would want Gary's kidney more than any other? I would have been happy to receive an elderly organ, one that would come to me in a mellow mood, without the rawness of a life cut unfairly short. I didn't have a chance to choose. I got what I was given, and I tried to make it work. What else have I ever done?

All the same, I can pinpoint the moment that was decisive, immunologically. It was actually before the operation, on that endless afternoon in the hospital, while I was gradually becoming aware of the staleness of my pyjamas. I was listening to the nurse talk about this mysterious biker who had taken his helmet off to make sure he was defenceless, had walked away from his machine and been hit by a van, and it struck me as inhuman that it was always 'he', 'him', 'the biker'. It was the merest scrap of dialogue, and I remember it well.

I said: 'Shouldn't you tell me what his name is? I'd feel more comfortable if I knew, somehow.'

She said: 'Absolutely not. I mustn't.'

Then I said: 'Don't you think it's silly to be squeamish about his name, when I'm not too squeamish to take his kidney, if I get the chance?'

And she smiled sadly, and she said: 'Well, you may have a point there.' Of course, they're always tired, they don't always know what they're doing. 'Gary,' she said. 'His name was Gary.'

That was all it took. I had asked her point-blank, but still I think she shouldn't have told me. I was in no mood to take no for an answer, but still it was her job to tell me no, however tired she was. It was obscene to tell me, obscene that she allowed me to know. At the moment that she spoke, the name was stitched into a waiting place in my brain. Gary's kidney. It was Gary's kidney, never mine.

All this was in my mind before the operation. Still, I managed to keep Terry's spirits up until it was time for my anaesthetic. And then I didn't have to think about anything at all for a while.

The holiday brochure came back with me from hospital, but I don't know what happened to it after that. Perhaps I stowed it away somewhere – I could just about have managed that – or perhaps it was Terry who thought it would be more tactful to keep it out of sight.

I hated being looked after. I hated Terry taking time off, without being able to use his travel privileges, the free flights that were the main consolation for the demeaning routines of his job. I felt he was being kept prisoner in a single time-zone. It wasn't fair on him.

It seems stupid to say that I hated him looking after me, and that I hated not looking after him, as if they were separate things. But that was how I felt. For the first time in fourteen years, I wasn't preparing the food he ate. The fridge seemed a long way away, and I didn't even know what was in it.

Gary's kidney was restless. Gary's kidney was out of its element. By this time the cyclosporine had been flowing so freely that the bloodstream bouncers were either actually unconscious or slumped stunned in the armchairs, and the whole place had been overrun by street people.

I have a memory of saying to Terry at one point – I was coughing a lot and I had a fever I couldn't seem to shake off – 'Do you remember that woman who used to send us Jehovah's Witness propaganda?'

All Terry would say was, 'Try not to talk.'

'Do you remember it was all about how you should refuse blood transfusions and trans-everything, because you'll need all your bits in one place come Judgement Day?'

'You're burning up, my babes. Try not to talk.'

'Don't keep saying that. Do you remember?'

'I remember.'

'Well I still say it's rubbish. Of course it's rubbish. But I think my body's beginning to see things her way.'

In fact the cough I was coughing turned out to be pneumonia, not the ordinary sort, the doctors didn't think, the sort people used to call the old man's friend, but a special sort that started befriending people on a large scale – young men at first, in fact – about ten years ago. This special kind of pneumonia, though, has always had a soft spot for people like me, people who have been softened up by cyclosporine. The bouncers had let it in with all the other riff-raff. It's called PCP. The initials stand for . . . well, the usual things initials stand for, names and technical terms that don't mean anything to lay people, which is why you use the initials.

For all I know they stand for Please Cough Painfully. Please Cough Porcupines. My chest felt like a porcupine sanctuary that needed more space. The poor spiny beasts in my lungs had no room to breathe. They were in danger of putting each other's eyes out with their quills, every time I took a breath.

I didn't understand what PCP was at first and I said, 'TCP? In the medicine cabinet, I think,' that being where we kept the antiseptics. I was a bit woozy, what with the pneumonia and everything. I really wasn't very lucid. Terry had to explain it to me. He told me they were taking me to a different hospital from the one where they gave me the kidney. This other hospital had a ward where PCP was something of a speciality of theirs.

I would have twigged a lot earlier if I hadn't been so sick. But when your chest feels like it's in a vice, your thoughts come in for their share of the squeezing. It was an Aids ward. Of course it was an Aids ward. It couldn't have been anything, really, but an Aids ward. And so it was that after such a long time of going my own way, I rejoined my generation in its place of special suffering.

I hadn't ever actually met anyone with Aids before, but you couldn't call it a social situation for the first few days. The new lot of doctors were too busy doing their little tests. One day they put me on an exercise bike – well, it was a little more technological than that, but that's what it amounted to – and they told me to pedal away on it so they could measure my oxygen saturation. They had me pedalling away with an electrode clipped to my ear. I felt like a cow with an ear tag condemned to hard labour in a health farm. They didn't even close the door, so anyone who cared to could watch me struggling away on that hellish saddle. Admittedly I was at the end of a corridor, but the principle's the same.

It felt like I was at the end of the line, and I wanted to be nearer the nurses' station, nearer to the heart of the ward. Except that Terry pointed out, if they have you near them, it's because they don't think you're going to make it.

I'll say one thing for the staff, they never treated me differently because I didn't have Aids. They didn't make me feel I was there under false pretences. They gave me the full works. Another time they sent a remote-control pair of scissors down my throat on a wire, so they could get a tissue sample. Then they seemed to get tired of testing me, and they let me alone for a while.

At times when my temperature was down and I could go for the occasional little wander, I started to take in some things about the workings of the ward. I noticed that biological family, old-fashioned next-of-kin, tended to visit at old-fashioned visiting hours – ten to twelve in the morning, two in the afternoon till eight in the evening – while at other times a small irregular army of lovers and semi-official functionaries seemed to have the run of the place. These unofficial or semi-official people seemed almost to supplement the staff. Sometimes the orthodox families were escorted, even cordoned off, by these intermediate people, as if the families were intruding in a place where they had no rights, and were only allowed in on condition of best behaviour.

There was a bizarre sense of community on the ward, verging at times on outright festivity. One tea-time, in a day room, I watched a glamorous magician in fishnet stockings, top hat and tails, who had started life as a boy and subsequently been a merchant seaman, do conjuring tricks for an audience most of whom were in wheelchairs, or trailing IV stands, or both. This appealing if transitional creature produced strings of handkerchiefs from the most unlikely places, from ears, from nostrils. Once she drew a string of handkerchiefs, to all appearances, from a sort of gauze-covered stopper mounted in someone's chest a little below the collarbone. This was an arrangement that made my little dialysis-fistula seem downright unenterprising in its meddling. It made possible injections straight into the heart.

The sick man's pyjama-top was open. He might almost have been showing off his chest with a horribly misplaced pride. As he grinned and the handkerchiefs emerged, as it seemed, from inside a chest whose every bone could have won a Knobbly Knees contest in a holiday camp, I felt for a dreamy moment that I had X-ray vision. I thought I could see the sick man's silted lungs as a shabby waistcoat, hanging from the wire coat-hanger of his shoulders, and his remaining life, in the form of a string of crusted hankies, being pulled from a pocket in the waistcoat by the nimble fingers of PCP.

The conjuror didn't choose me as the subject of any of her tricks. I experienced a groggy adult version of the exclusion that I would have felt if the same thing had happened at a children's party when I was four or five. On that ward I felt different from my fellow patients, not superior, believe me, but different. It wasn't that I thought I was innocent. It absolutely wasn't that. I thought I was irrelevant.

On examination, from what I could see over people's shoulders, the handkerchiefs that the conjuror had produced so deftly turned out to have been embroidered, rather neatly, near the hem, with the motto *Tears are for sissies*, perhaps by the same chunky but eye-deceiving hands that had worked the vanishes and disappearances. Perhaps I was delirious. Perhaps that didn't happen. Between you and me, I've been on the receiving end of a certain amount of morphine since then, and morphine seems to go in for some embroidering on its own account.

Another day, while I was waiting for Terry to arrive, a nurse popped her head round the door and asked if I felt well enough for art class. They were very big on making the time pass, on that ward. I wasn't at all sure I was up to it, but she promised to bring me back if I didn't feel well enough after all, and I thought I'd give it a try. I think I managed to say, 'What the hell. Let's live a little.' I wasn't steady on my feet, and she helped me along the corridor to the day room.

A few patients were already busy drawing; they didn't look up from their work. The art master, or art-based social worker if that's what he was, patted my shoulder very gently and gave me some cartridge paper and some crayons. There were some freesias in a glass of water on the table, and I got down to trying to sketch them. I thought that was the way an art class worked. Every now and then I was aware of the teacher coming up behind one of the other patients and murmuring 'Very good,' or even 'I'm proud of you,' sometimes giving them a careful brotherly shoulder-hug from behind to underline the praise.

One of my fellow students was in a wheelchair. His legs were wrapped in bandages. Unless the bandages were very thick and were wrapped round him many times – and I could see no advantage to that – his legs were hugely swollen. Another of our little group of amateur artists had hung his cane on the back of his chair. He was sticking his tongue out as he sketched, the way schoolboys do when they're concentrating. The inherently hopeful gesture made for a strange contrast with a whitened patch on the top of his ear. It made me think of frostbite, which doesn't mean much because I don't really know what frostbite looks like.

When the teacher or counsellor or whatever he was came and stood behind me I started to get very self-conscious. I suppose I was waiting for my hug, wanting it but also braced against it, and the waiting made me nervous. I said, 'I don't think I've got that yellow quite right,' just to have something to say, and then at last he made physical contact, not a hug, though, a very tentative pat.

'It's okay to let go of your feelings, you know,' he said. 'You don't have to keep everything in.' I didn't think I had particular feelings about freesias, though they are a pretty flower, but when he let me have a look at the other drawings, the drawings that had earned hugs, I saw what he meant.

My fellow artists had used only the black crayon. One of them had drawn a skinny figure holding on to a cliff-face with its fingernails, and another had drawn a skinny figure screaming while being flushed down a lavatory. I suppose, looking back on it, that my pathetically cheerful freesias must have looked like the very freesias of denial, but still I would have felt like a fake trying my hand at the expressionism that seemed to be what was wanted. My conversation with mortality had started too early, and gone on too long, for that style of cry to feel right to me.

Then Terry came in, and he seemed very upset. He wasn't interested in anyone's drawing. He was almost rude. It took me a while before I realized what the matter was. On that ward, there was only one, unwritten rule, and I had broken it. I had left my room without leaving a note on the door to say where I was. It was incredibly thoughtless. I couldn't blame Terry for being upset, for being pretty much beside himself.

After a while he calmed down a bit, and he even helped me with a bit of artwork. I wanted a sign to put on my door. It was to show a dog-collar crossed out with a diagonal red line, only it isn't easy to draw a dog-collar just hanging there, without a neck. What the sign meant, obviously, was *No Priests*. No God-botherers.

Terry didn't ask me why I wanted the sign, why I couldn't just send people away. I could feel him not asking me. I couldn't tell him the reason. I couldn't tell him I was afraid that Vicar Bob would turn up sooner or later. I dreaded that one day I would hear the creak of his caring shoes.

On a good day I could cope with him. On a good day I was more than up to that. But on a bad day I might not have the speed to interrupt him, when he started on one of those sentences that said, 'I'm not speaking as a priest now William . . .' He might have put his hand on my hand, and I wasn't having that.

A couple of days after the art class I would have made a better shot at a melodramatic sketch, except that I would hardly have been able to hold a crayon. I even got my wish to be closer to the nurses' station, closer to the heart of the ward. By that time, I well and truly belonged.

There's a cycle, you see, of infection and medication. It's swings and roundabouts – but swings and roundabouts in some nightmare inner-city playground, where there's broken glass on the swings and dogshit on the roundabouts. You cut the cyclosporine, to wake the bouncers up, and they clear the room of riff-raff . . .

and intimidate the kidney. So you boost the cyclosporine instead, and the bouncers pass out again. Only it turns out all the low life has just been lurking on the stairs. They shuffle back in, him among them, street person with staring eyes, rattling his Aids collection box. Collecting for Aids, always Aids.

I opened my eyes. The sleep they give you in hospital isn't the real thing, it's always a placebo. Somebody else must be getting the real thing, but you're only part of the control group. You can open your eyes from placebo-sleep and close them a moment later, laying down a fresh deposit of sleepy-dust before you have time to wipe away the grains of the last unconsciousness.

I opened my eyes again. Then I half-closed them, so I could watch Terry from under the lids. He was eating a grape from a bunch on the bedside table. Terry looked terrible, haggard and worn, but it was the bunch of grapes that really shocked me. It had the look of a bunch of grapes picked at by toddlers. There was no pattern to Terry's feeding. He didn't choose grapes in a logical way, pulling off a clump, for instance, and eating all of it, or clearing a stem and then its neighbour. He was nibbling, and nibbling at random.

I felt I could hear the controlled explosions of juice as Terry bit down. I didn't think of asking for a grape or two myself, dry as I was. I knew they would feel like marbles in my mouth.

Whenever Terry touched the dish with a finger, he'd do a nervous little five-finger exercise on it with all the other fingers, a neurotic strum, as if he was a child just beginning to play the piano. Such a trivial thing to notice, yet it was only then that it hit me. I had been in poor health for so long, it had somehow slipped my mind that after all that time on the edge it was still possible to fall off the map. I closed my eyes again.

Aids, HTLV3, HIV – however you wish to be known. I must give you your due. I need to acknowledge what I owe. Without you and the changes you have made, my Terry would never have found the courage to sit on the bed and to hold me. To begin with, he leaned carefully against me and kept his feet on the floor. Then he shyly lifted one leg on to the bed, keeping the other toe still in cautious contact with the floor, and with a weather eye on the nurses' station to see if they disapproved. After a little while, he was sufficiently encouraged by their implied permission – they probably hadn't noticed his little experiment in affection – to lift both legs clear of the floor and lie full length by my side. His warm front felt cool against my hot back.

I went to sleep next to someone I knew, and I woke side by side with a stranger. He was under the sheet. I had no memory of Terry being quite so bold. The person lying next to me was turned on his side, facing away from me. I reached out a hand under the sheets and touched bare flesh – warm skin and the edge of material, a woollen waistband. My hand knew with electrical certainty who and what it touched. It was Peter Hunter. *Peter Hunter*. It was Peter Hunter. It was the small of Peter Hunter's back, just above the curve of the buttocks.

Carefully I pulled the sheet away from him, and got a shock. Peter Hunter had a pony-tail. Without thinking, I raised a hand to it. I didn't pull at it, not at all, but it came away in my hand. I'd always wanted to know what keeps those things on – what are they called, hair extensions? – and the answer seems to be, nothing much.

I looked around for somewhere to put this embarrass-ing trophy. I reached across and opened the drawer of the bedside table as quietly as I could. A little to my surprise, it was empty. I leaned over and slipped Peter Hunter's little hair-piece out of sight.

I was just getting used to Peter Hunter being there. My hand wandered down his back beneath the sheet, to where I had first touched him. I couldn't help myself. Then my hand found something else that was a shock, a patch of skin with a raised texture. All I could think of was that this was a kidney scar like mine, a wound marking the place where an organ was taken. Then I realized that this patch had a rough texture, unlike the unearthly smoothness of scar tissue. I peeled back the sheet so I could see. It was a tattoo, of a little hank of red ribbon. I noticed that some of the red had come off on my fingers, and as gently as I could I gave the tattoo a rub.

The design smudged and came away on my hands. It was only temporary, and it came off in flakes and crumbs. It left no more trace than if Peter Hunter had been eating biscuits in bed. In my bed.

I wiped my hands on the sheet and then covered him

up with it again. I touched the skin of his neck, next to where the pony-tail had been. Peter Hunter was very hot. I made room for him and rolled him gently on to his back. He didn't stir. Then I set out to find something to cool him down. I found I was much steadier on my feet than I had any reason to expect, but then looking after someone else is the best way of getting your problems in proportion, isn't that what they say? And this wasn't just anybody. This was *Peter Hunter*.

There was a flannel in the basin that Terry had been using to wipe my face before he left, to go wherever he went. I turned on the tap and waited for the water to run as cold as it would ever get, which in hospita' is never very cold.

That's the funny thing about hospital. The radiators are never quite on or off. The food is never quite hot. The lights are never quite bright. The radio is never quite loud. Your temperature is never quite down.

Everything says in a quiet separate voice: This is a place of in-between. Sleep is never quite deep. Consciousness is never quite sharp, and the taps never run quite cold.

I squeezed the flannel out in the water a few times, and went back to the bed. I passed the cool cloth as gently as I could over Peter Hunter's face. He didn't open his eyes, but he slowly swivelled his big neck to follow the flannel as I moved it, and he half-opened his mouth. I hesitated, and then I stopped moving the flannel, and I let Peter Hunter find it with his mouth. Still his eyes were shut, but he drew a good length of the damp cloth into his mouth. His lips closed slowly round it, and I could sense his tongue working to mash out all the moistness and refreshment that it held.

He was still very hot to the touch. Gently I pulled the blanket away from him. He wasn't wearing anything above the waist. The flesh of his midriff was full and smooth and tanned. Below that I could see what looked like an incongruously thick woollen waistband, in a tartan design. Carefully, not wanting to wake him, I pulled the blanket down as far as his knees. Peter Hunter was wearing a kilt.

No wonder he was hot. Thick as it was, the material was wet through. He might almost have pissed himself. I took the liberty of unfastening the pin that held Peter Hunter's kilt in place. It was like a big silver safety-pin. Once the kilt was unpinned, I thought it would just come loose, as if it was only a big bandage, but it turned out to be wrapped round his hips many times. I tugged tentatively at the material, hoping to free it without waking Peter Hunter.

He stirred, but only to raise his hips a little from the bed, as if he was giving permission for me to unwrap him. I unwound the cloth as gently as I could. When I had completed one turn, and had a considerable amount of damp tartan in my hands, Peter Hunter raised his hips again. Unless I was imagining it, this time he twisted his pelvis ever so slightly as he raised it from the sheet, as if he was entertaining a memory of pleasure. As I gathered the cloth that I was holding into folds, it struck me that I recognized the tartan. It was predominantly blue and green, and it wasn't just any tartan. It was Hunting Stewart.

My head was buzzing with heat and thinking. Just as if I was looking at a Peter Hunter magazine and trying to deduce its hidden meanings, I started to wonder if this was another sly game, this time a visual pun. Peter Hunter wearing Hunting Stewart. Was he trying to tell me that his real name, before he changed it for professional purposes, was *Stewart* Hunter? Then I almost laughed. This wasn't a magazine. Peter Hunter was here. I only had to ask him when he woke up.

When I had unravelled two full turns of plaid from Peter Hunter's hips, and the end of the kilt was not yet in sight, Peter Hunter stopped helping me to unwrap him. I tugged at the material, but Peter Hunter made no further effort to raise his hips. He rested his full weight on the slyly hinting kilt. Perhaps he was asleep again. I was tired now from my efforts, and I sat back down on the bed.

I took the dog back. I don't know that it was wrong. I didn't want Terry to have her any more. 'Baby come to Papa,' I said. She wagged her tail. Good girl.

Before we left the house I wanted her to fetch me something. She was a retriever, wasn't she? Then let her retrieve. What I wanted was kept in my bedroom. It wasn't any part of the Peter Hunter archive, which she could hardly be expected to drag bodily from the premises. In any case I didn't mind Terry finding the archive. There was nothing there, really, that would surprise him. The archive lived in my room, but it was part of our life for all that.

What I was after was different. It was small enough for Lacquer to hold in her mouth. It was kept in a drawer, by a happy chance more or less at the level of a Labrador's jaws. It was a chest of drawers that I inherited from my Mum, a nice piece, the only thing that I would have been tempted to drag along to the *Antiques Roadshow*, if it had come to our neck of the woods, to see what the experts said. The trouble was that the handles on the drawers were hinged, and Lacquer couldn't get a decent purchase.

I'd be urging her on, and she'd just be able to nose the handle up to near-horizontal, but then she wouldn't be able to consolidate her grip. Well obviously she couldn't. If dogs could do that they wouldn't be dogs. Every time she tried it the handle, wet with her drool, would slip back to where it had started. Then she'd look up pleadingly to where I was, hoping not to have to try again, hoping to be allowed to go out.

So in the end I had to leave it behind, the packet of snapshots I had taken of Terry over the years, without him having the least idea about it. Terry was a martyr to his little cock. He was so busy being a martyr to his cock that he never gave a thought to his other assets. A good deal of the time he was sitting on them.

The snapshots I had snatched over the years, from far enough away that he didn't know I was there with my camera, were of Terry from behind – Terry in acetate shorts laying a rockery, Terry in torn jeans dead-head-ing. He never knew how much I appreciated his pretty arse, less in bed than out of it. In the envelope there was even a picture of Terry squatting down to pat Lacquer's head, when she was a puppy.

I had to leave the envelope behind. If Lacquer had managed to open the drawer I would have got her to drop it somewhere away from the house, down a drain maybe, or to bury it if she was in a digging mood. Sometimes she liked to dig. But after ten minutes of trying to turn her tongue into a finger for my benefit, she'd had enough. She was bored, and she was mad to be out of doors. It was just beginning to get light, and I had my own reasons for not wanting to wait too long. We needed to be outside before it was full day.

It took her another ten minutes to work the catch on the bathroom window. She whined a little while she worked at it, because the most mechanically efficient lever, her nose, was also one of her most tender parts, and it hurt her to keep on pushing. Finally she did it. The window swung open and we were outside, on a treacherous slope of cold wet grass.

I tried to make Lacquer sit in the road right away, but she wasn't having any of that. She wanted her usual walk, and the fullest form of it at that, no short cuts. She insisted on the whole canal loop as the reward for her hard work, complete with browsing and pauses for territorial peeing. Like so many spayed bitches she had developed a modified style of urination, involving something remarkably like the cocking of a leg. She liked to mark, as a dog would. On the way back she stopped at the newsagents, which wasn't yet open, but I think she was only doing that to tease me.

Even then, properly exercised as she was, she didn't want to Sit for me. She would only do the pretend Sit I knew of old, just bending her hind legs until I'd moved off a bit, and then straightening up to follow me.

Finally she consented to Sit properly, but even then she had to have her own way. She wouldn't set her haunches down anywhere near the road surface, but luckily she could be persuaded to Sit on the slightly raised surface of a mini-roundabout, the built-up white disc that traffic is supposed to circulate around. Of course traffic does nothing of the sort, least of all in the early morning, when the mortgage-squeezed yuppies start their daily migration, so for my purposes it was quite as good as if she'd sat down in the road itself. She liked the shallow-domed hub of the mini-roundabout so much that she staked a claim to it in her own way, with her urine. Then I knew that she would really Sit, and Stay.

I wasn't really punishing Terry by taking away his source of comfort. It was a little more honest than that. I was punishing her directly. When I bought Lacquer for Terry it was a loving gesture, but it was also a grievous mistake. We both realized as much soon enough, though we didn't talk about it. We didn't have to. Lacquer was my second great gift to Terry, and it cancelled out the first. Things could never be the same after that.

It may be there had always been an element of play-acting involved. I would come into Terry's bedroom with the tea-tray as quietly as possible. I wouldn't open the curtains or put a light on. I'd pour out two cups in the near-dark, and put one softly on the table next to the bed. Then I'd take a good slurp from my cup, as soon as it was cool enough to drink at all. I would hold the tea in my mouth for an interval that had to be carefully judged. It was no part of the plan to boil Terry alive, after all. Once I was satisfied that the moment was right, I would gently peel back the duvet and go to wake Terry with my mouth.

It wasn't a dispensable ritual of our life together, that I should rouse Terry there, just there, where he felt least of a man. And after Lacquer arrived, our ritual was spoiled. It may be that the clink of the tea things some-times woke Terry, although he didn't let on. It may even be that Terry was never taken by surprise, and was always pretending to be asleep. That's not the point. After Lacquer arrived, everything was different. How-ever quietly I crept into the room, she would give a little growl at the back of her throat. It wasn't the sort of growl she'd have made for an intruder, it wasn't in the least a sign of aggression. It was dutiful – it was part of Labrador software – and it went with a wag of the tail. But it was loud enough to make it absurd for Terry to go on pretending to be asleep.

Of course we went on with our ritual, but it wasn't the same. Sometimes Lacquer would jump up on to the bed, and then we'd have to stop what we were doing. But even if she kept her distance, it was all spoiled.

We were only pretending for each other's benefit that everything was as it had been before she came.

It's not an easy trick to do well, the hot-tea blow-job. Terry will never find anyone with a technique to match mine. And if love is measured by its cost, there was a lot of love in that morning gesture, repeated so many times along the years. A teacup of average size contains five fluid ounces. Waking Terry as he loved to be woken would cost me 20 per cent of my daily ration, in the dialysis years. A full fifth of what I could drink in a day.

I took the dog back, and I can't say I'm sorry. But when did I do that? I must ask Peter Hunter. Perhaps he'll remember. Perhaps he has the answers.

Peter Hunter hasn't said more than a few words, but in another way, he's told me a lot. His accent turns out to be English, which explains quite a few things. In a way I should blame him for coming to this country for free treatment, when he has enough money to pay American medical bills, if anyone in the world does. But he was entitled – he must have kept dual nationality – and I don't have the heart to disapprove.

I feel rather a fool, now, not to have read any of the interviews in the magazines that were among my proudest possessions. Fancy having a complete collection of Hunteriana, and never suspecting for a moment that my idol was British!

When Peter Hunter opened his eyes at last, I gave him a big smile and went back to unwrapping the kilt. He let me do it for a few moments, and then it was as if he suddenly remembered something horrible. He sat bolt upright in bed, and he grabbed hold of the edge of the material, just as I was finally about to pull it away from him. Remembering that Scotsmen don't wear anything under the kilt, I thought he was having a belated attack of modesty, which seemed a bit rich, all things considered. But it wasn't that. For one thing, he was wearing underpants, rather dowdy cellular underpants at that, the sort of thing that Terry used to wear when I first met him. But quite apart from that, it wasn't his modesty that he was defending.

Peter Hunter seemed to take a deep breath, and then slowly peeled the edge of the material away from his thighs. He frowned and then his face cleared. He ran his fingers in wonderment over unblemished skin.

Then, without so much as a glance at me, Peter Hunter pulled down his dowdy underpants, yanking them down over his thick grey socks. He looked down at his genitals, and then he started pulling them fiercely this way and that, peeling back the little familiar foreskin, feeling his scrotum with unbelieving fingertips. Finally his touch became less frantic, and he drew a few deep breaths, to calm himself down.

I have to say his cock doesn't look as big as it does in the pictures, no bigger than mine in fact. Of course cock size means nothing to me, never has, but perhaps that ugly contraption the vacuum pump had its uses after all. It must be quite some time since he had a chance to use one.

Finally Peter Hunter started staring at his feet, as if they were very far away from him, and then looking at me with an unmistakably pleading expression. I felt that I knew what he meant by that look. 'Do you want me to take your socks off for you?' I asked, and he just swallowed and nodded, as if any horror in the world might be revealed by this final unwrapping.

I pull at both socks at once – there seems no point in prolonging the agony – and all that is revealed is an embarrassingly cheesy odour. Peter Hunter tries to look at the soles of both his feet at the same time, which is close to being a physical impossibility, and then he runs his hands hysterically over them. It takes him quite some time to be satisfied that his feet are smooth and perfect. He is naked now, and he bursts at last into tears.

I wish I could tell you that I like it when men cry. I sit down on the bed, but I can't bring myself to touch Peter Hunter just yet. After a while, the snuffling dies down, and I feel his warm hand on the small of my back. He pulls me gently towards him, and I let myself be drawn down till I am lying by his side, with my back to him. I feel the wet approach of his tongue at my ear. He is surprisingly unskilful with his tongue, as if all he could manage with it was a basic lapping motion, nothing more pointed. He doesn't seem to want to put his tongue inside my ear, just to lick away at the outside of it. He stops, and immediately my ear feels cold, as Peter Hunter's saliva starts to evaporate. I can feel him gathering breath to speak. It is as if he is drawing up from that noble throat a single sentence that will express everything he has been through, everything we have both been through to reach this point in our lives. Behind me on the bed he releases his breath into meaning, and he says, with complete conviction, 'Let's eat Italian.'